The Knife I Carry

A Lightwalkers Novel

Jacquelyn Holmes

Titles by Jacquelyn Holmes

Lightwalker Novels
Lightwalkers
The Knife I Carry

Native Legends
Rabbit-Trapped
The Thrown-Away Son
Twisted Hearts

A
LIGHTWALKERS
NOVEL

THE
KNIFE
I
CARRY

JACQUELYN HOLMES

Library of Congress Control Number: 2026908591

ISBN: 979-8-9918157-8-9

Parental Advisory:

This story contains elements of suicidal ideation that may not be appropriate for all readers.

If you or someone you know is struggling with suicidal thoughts, please find help.

Call 988 for the National Suicide and Crisis Lifeline

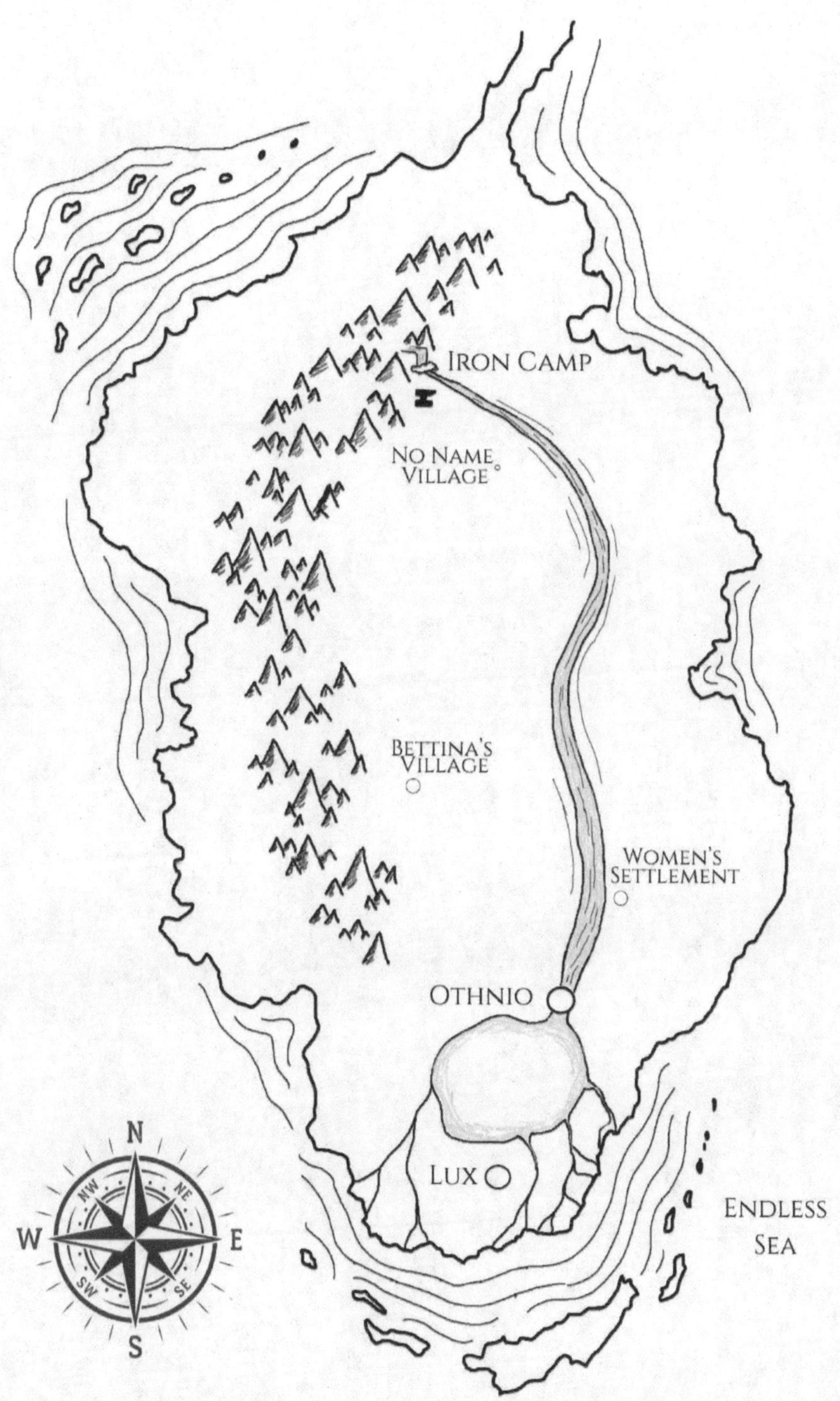

Iron Camp
No Name Village
Bettina's Village
Women's Settlement
Othnio
Lux
Endless Sea
N
NW
NE
W
E
SW
SE
S

Part One

Chapter One

Roll left.

Without question, I did, diving left, onto my shoulder and rolling back up to my feet. In the place where I had been sitting, there was a notch in the bark of the tree where a rock had hit.

I looked up, already grinning. There was only one person in the world who would throw a rock at the back of my head unprovoked.

"Heva!" I exclaimed, running to hug my older sister around the waist. An answering smile was on her lips, though she tried to mold them into something sterner. She took me by the shoulders and pushed me back.

"Let me have a look at you, Cunigast," she said, pretending to frown. "Tell me the truth, did I hit you?"

I shook my head, and smiled. The Voice had told me what to do, as it often did. I didn't say anything about that to Heva though, not since that first time last year. She told me to keep it to myself, so I did. I did most everything Heva asked me to do.

Heva's fingers searched my scalp, checking for injuries. She'd thrown the rock hard, and I supposed she expected me to have a lump. I always smiled, even when she did hit me, so that was no indicator.

"Come," she said, her hand coming to rest on my shoulder. "It's time to head back home."

Heva turned and began walking. I lengthened my strides to keep up with her.

"What were you doing out here, so far from the others?" she asked, not looking back. Heva had long black hair that she wore in two braids. They were pulled forward over her shoulders, and were so shiny that they glistened in the sun. I had been thumped behind my ears more than once for pulling on them. At eighteen, Heva would soon be assigned a fiance. She would leave and join another household, leaving me behind with our father. I swallowed the lump that grew in my throat every time I thought about it.

I was eight years old, and the idea of spending the next ten years alone with Da seemed unimaginable. Up until now, I'd never spent more than a half hour in my father's presence. Now I was facing years. Even a week with him sounded like a nightmare, but years? What alternative did I have, though? I didn't dare run away.

"I was practicing my cuts on the leaves," I said proudly. So far, my light hadn't come in as strongly as the others my age. I saw my father looking at me sideways often, and I knew he was wondering why I struggled where others succeeded.

If I weren't excelling in other areas, the elders would have probably assumed I was born deficient. So far, even the other kids with the highest light production could not land a hit on me during a sparring session. They didn't know it was because Heva had trained me relentlessly almost from birth.

They didn't know how much the Voice helped me, either. I didn't dare speak about that.

"How is your control?" she asked.

"I guess it's as good as anybody's," I answered with a shrug. Using light to cut leaves was a bit like using a sword to cut your bread.

"And your light production? Do you need to share?" she asked. I was too young to have a light partner, and I generally just shared with Heva or Da. Heva should have taken a light partner some time ago, but for reasons I didn't understand, she had not. I didn't care. Given the choice, I'd have taken Heva over anyone else.

"I need to be topped up," I answered, my shoulders slumping. It was a common enough problem for me, and one that shamed me. I almost never gave light to anyone. Instead, I needed Heva to feed light back to me, or I wouldn't last through the night.

In answer, she held her arm out, and I gripped it with my own. There was the immediate tingling sensation between us, and the trickle of light. She fed it to me slowly so that it didn't burn, and she knew exactly when to stop. I felt the light travelling outward toward my fingers and toes. There was a small sense of Heva in that light, an awareness of who it belonged to.

I didn't mind that either. It was infinitely preferable to sharing with my father.

At home, we entered the cabin well before long shadows were settling in. Unlike some of my peers, I had to be mindful of the shadows. I often didn't have enough light to do more than keep myself alive. None to spare for scaring off the shadow creatures that came out after dark. It was those shapeless monsters that we trained our whole lives through to fight against. They could only be dispersed with light, and we Lightwalkers could shed light from our skin as if it came directly from our bones. How Lightwalkers could do this was a mystery that even the elders didn't know. We only knew that we could, and therefore must, or the world would be overrun with shadow creatures.

In front of the cabin, Da was stoking up the fire. He was bent over and I could see little of his expression. At his side, there was a rough-hewn table and food was piled there, waiting for us to prepare. Heva went to it, and started sorting what she would use tonight and what needed to be put back in the house. I watched her keep the potatoes and set back the squash and corn. A large side of venison and an onion stayed. My belly growled.

I took the armful of vegetables she set in her discard pile and towed them into the cabin. It was a rough, wooden structure with only a single room inside. Our beds were tucked to the right, and a thick rug filled the space to the left. At the back of the cabin there were two more tables and a short row of shelves. I deposited the vegetables there, next to a wheel of cheese and the bread Heva had baked yesterday.

Who was going to feed us once Heva got married? I didn't know how to bake, and I'd never once seen Da do it. Just one more reason to dread my sister's engagement, I supposed.

"Where were you, boy?" Da asked the moment I stepped out of the cabin again.

"In the woods," I answered. It's where I spent most of my free time.

"Doing what?" he asked. His voice came out as thick and hard as gravel. I hadn't answered him correctly.

"I was practicing my cutting," I said, shrugging.

"Could have done that right here at home, boy," Da answered, rising to his feet. "No reason to make your sister come hunt you down every night."

I nodded my head, acknowledging his words, even as I knew I'd do it again.

He disappeared into the cabin, and I looked at Heva. She had diced up vegetables and now had a stewpot cooking over the fire. The light from the fire set her hair and eyes to shining, and I wondered if that's what our mother would have looked like, standing over the fire.

"Heva, do you have to get married?" I ask, sidling up next to her. "I think me and Da will starve if you're not here to feed us."

Instead of answering, she ruffled my hair. I ducked away, shrugging off her hand. She did that a lot lately, touch me. She was always gripping my shoulder or messing with my hair. More than once, I'd caught her staring at me with a strange look in her eyes. I didn't know why, but I suspected it had something to do with her upcoming marriage.

"Just remember you don't have to be like him, Gast," Heva says. "You don't have to be so hard."

Chapter Two

The camp elders deemed Heva suitable for marriage, and arranged for her to marry a boy from within our own camp. I didn't know him, but Heva did. His name was Roderic, and he was as tall as she was, though his hair wasn't as dark. Together, they looked like a pair of hunting birds, honed to a knife's edge and ready to fly. I stood next to her while she said her vows, and wondered if this fellow, Roderic, was going to take her away from me forever.

Da stood outside the circle while she was wed, and after it was over, he drug me away by my shoulder without even bothering to say goodbye.

I cried that night, certain I would starve to death without her.

As I suspected, Da didn't know how to bake. The first week after Heva married, I wasn't convinced he knew how to cook at all. Together, we stumbled through our meals. More often than not, I went to bed with a grumbling belly. It looked more and more like a slow death at my father's side.

But I didn't starve. I hadn't understood that Heva wouldn't be going on runs anymore.

Every Lightwalker went on at least one run in their life. It was a long trip by horseback into the down lands, to hunt breachers. A shadow creature could sometimes turn into a breacher, which was much more dangerous. A breacher didn't have any more shape than a shadow creature, but it took on *mass*. They could pull a tree up, roots and all, and throw them. They could change their shape at will to have two, three, or more arms, each one just as strong as the first. And a breacher set loose amongst people? Well, it didn't bear thinking how many souls could be stolen away or left hollowed before such a creature could be killed by a Lightwalker's light flare.

And then there were daybreakers. But thank the Gods Above that no one had seen one of those in a generation or more.

While every Lightwalker was required to go on at least one run in their life, many never went on a second. Heva had trained and trained to go on runs, so I had assumed she would continue. But now that she was married, she had decided to focus on her knifemaking instead. And since she'd married within our own camp, she could still come and visit me. Twice a week, she came to our cabin with a couple of loaves of bread in tow.

"Have to keep up your training, Gast," she would say, then drag me off into the woods.

Training with Heva was always head and shoulders above what I received in camp with the other kids. She had an intensity that I could never fully understand.

"Let's go again," she said, a layer of sweat on her brow. Today, she tied my left arm up against my side so that I couldn't move it at all.

"Why are we doing this? My arm works!" I moaned, trying and failing to break my arm free.

"We're doing this because if you are fighting a breacher, and it hollows your arm, you have to keep fighting so you don't lose your life as well. Do you want to die?" she asked, deadly serious.

"Of course not, but if I lose an arm, I will probably die in the seconds after, won't I?"

Instead of answering, Heva bared her teeth at me. It was past the time for questions. I took up my knife just in time. She lunged, coming at me with her knife bared. I dodged and turned, avoiding the knife's edge, but my bound arm slowed me down.

Drop down. Roll right. I did as the Voice said, and avoided a wicked move my sister favored. I'd seen her execute it on others a hundred times, but she'd never used it on me.

"Are you trying to hurt me for real?" I shouted. I'd just had my ninth birthday, and I found that I was angry all of the time. It simmered under the surface of my skin, waiting to burst free.

I had been forced to take light from Da since Heva was gone, and I was afraid that his dark moods were infecting me through the light we shared. I hated it, and I hated myself for needing it.

Heva threw her knife down, suddenly just as angry as I was.

"Don't you see, Gast? If you aren't the best at this, they will leave you behind!"

Her voice echoed against the trees, and I struggled to get my breath back. The birds had quieted. I imagined her words ricocheting up into the canopy, then the sky, until they reached the very stars where the Gods were said to live.

"You don't make enough light," she said, and looked away. "You'll have to be the very best at everything else if you're going to stand a chance."

"You mean at getting married?" I asked, aghast. "I don't want some girl to take care of anyway. I'll just come live with you."

"You can't, Gast-" she choked on her words, and I realized she was crying.

"Why not? I'll work. I'll help. I'll even be nice to Roderic. If you have kids, I'll help them, too. I don't care!" I shouted. The anger was swelling inside me. "Just as long as I don't have to live with Da forever."

"Haven't you wondered why the council hasn't made Da marry again?" Her voice was quiet, and I lowered mine, too.

"What? He already married once. He had us. Isn't that enough?"

"He's still young, Gast. He could have remarried and had more children. But he didn't. And it isn't because he loved our mother so much," she said.

The words speared me like one of her sharp knives. I winced. I didn't remember our mother, but I liked to imagine

that she was something special. I liked to imagine that my
father was special, too. That maybe it was losing her that had
turned him into who he was now.

"Then why?" I threw my own knife down. It stuck
point down in the dirt next to hers.

"Light production. Da doesn't produce much more
than you do. The council doesn't want him passing that on to
any more children. They don't want any more *like us*, Gast."

I felt the impact of those words like a blow to the
stomach.

"But you share with me all the time. So does Da now,"
I said, trying to make sense.

"I know. I did. I still will. But, Gast. I was going to the
healer tents to load up almost daily. I don't have enough for
myself. It's part of why they gave me to Roderic. He has
plenty to spare," she answered, color staining her cheeks
even darker.

She was ashamed.

The truth stopped up my throat, and slithered down
my belly until it lodged itself somewhere in my guts. Our
family didn't produce enough light. Our family wasn't good
enough. And if Heva was going to the healer tents to get

enough light to get through a day, then what had Da been doing? Whose light had I been taking?

Chapter Three

By the time I turned ten, I stopped taking light from my father. Instead, I went directly to the healer tents myself. There was always a willing Lightwalker there, ready to share with a stranger. It was part of their work, to share with any of us that needed it. Still, my cheeks burned with shame every time I went.

Taking light from a healer was like getting sunshine fed directly into my veins. It didn't feel like it was going to infect me with darkness, like it did when I took from my father.

Heva continued to train me, until she had her own children. Roderic was a good father, and his children gave off enough light that Heva's children would be accepted well into our camp society. I was happy for her, even if it took her more and more away from me.

By the time Heva had to quit my training altogether, I was able to hold my own in a fight with boys years older than myself. I couldn't produce enough light to get through a day, but I was deadly with a knife.

The other skills were there as well. By the time I was twelve, I could start a fire under any condition, track game through any wood, and find my way through the blackest night. I had taken Heva's words to heart. I was the best at everything that didn't have to do with light production.

It changed nothing.

I pushed my way through the crowd at the square and ignored the looks I caught from those I brushed against. Adults sneering down at me like it was my fault breachers existed in the world. I swallowed back curses and ducked my head low.

Heva was in the square with her children, each small enough to get lost in a crowd like this. I didn't see Roderic anywhere. He was often gone from camp, as a trader and courier between the various Lightwalker camps. She saw me and waved me over. I wedged myself in next to her oldest boy, Osuin. Tucking his hand into my own, I anchored him in place. Heva had Rada, her daughter, on her hip and Helm, her second oldest, was tugging on her hand.

They had called us here for some big announcement. I only knew to come because Heva had spotted me late yesterday and told me about it. I suspected no one cared if I came or not.

The man at my side jostled against me, then recoiled when he saw who I was. I narrowed my eyes at him, only just refraining from baring my teeth.

It's not catching, I thought. That's how they often acted, as if my low light production were contagious.

Serg stood tall at the central brazier, and he flashed his light once, bright and quick, but enough to catch everyone's attention. That familiar simmer of jealousy in the pit of my stomach.

"I gathered you here to meet the newest additions to Iron Camp!" Serg called, raising his hands. Curious eyes were jockeying for a better glimpse of the individuals standing at Serg's shoulder.

From my place I could see little more than the tops of heads. Some enterprising individual thought to bring a box, and a dark face appeared above the crowd.

He smiled broadly, a warm smile that I couldn't imagine on my own father's face.

"Thank you for the warm welcome to your community!"

I wondered what had brought him here. It wasn't unheard of for Lightwalkers to change camps, but I hadn't known anyone to do it.

"Where did he come from?" I asked Heva. She was tugging Helm back from the people closest to her and could only spare a shrug in my direction.

"Horse camp, I think?" she muttered.

The dark man's face disappeared and was replaced by a pale beauty. She had hair almost blonde in color. I wondered if that's what downlander hair looked like. I'd heard they sometimes even had *red* hair, if such a tale could be believed.

"Thank you for welcoming me and my family," she said, her voice didn't carry as well as her husband's. Still, her cheeks pinked up and I thought she looked kind. She probably wouldn't hiss and recoil if I walked across her shadow, would she?

Osuin tugged on my hand. I looked down and he put his arms up to me.

"The view isn't much better here," I said, but obligingly raised him up to sit on my shoulders. He stuck his baby fingers in my ears and I winced. I peeled them back, and tickled his chunky legs. He was giggling, his sticky fingers in my hair. I'd almost forgotten about the new family at the front.

Then *she* appeared. The box wasn't enough to boost her small stature up into view, so her father perched her up on his shoulder. She was smiling, her coloring high and her eyes snapping bright.

"I'm Eusebia!" she called, and I had no trouble hearing that clear voice. "Nice to meet you!"

There was a scattering of laughter through the crowd, not unkind. Her hair was almost as light as her mother's, though her skin wasn't so strangely pale. She was tawny like a mountain cat, and just as comfortable up on her high perch. I fancied the sun liked her as much as I did, the way she glowed like an ember in the afternoon shine.

Without thinking, I pulled Osuin down and passed him back to Heva. Then I drifted through the crowd, wedging myself between adults until I was looking up at the girl still in her father's arms. She was smiling like she'd never known a sad day in her life. I felt her beauty and joy like the glimmer of light on a knife's edge. It was sharp and painful, but I couldn't look away from her.

Gods Above, I want to... I didn't know how to finish the thought. I wanted to what? Speak to her? The very idea sent a shiver through me and made my palms sweaty.

"There you are," a voice said at my shoulder, followed by a heavy hand. It spun me around and the sight of the girl was replaced by my father's frowning face. I recoiled, not unlike that man had done to me only a few moments ago. My father saw it and dropped his hand.

"Get back to the cabin. Only taking up space here, boy," he said. I followed him through the crowd. It was like following him down into a dark hole.

Why couldn't I stay like everyone else?

"Best for everyone if you two stay home," a voice hissed. I turned, fists already curled up tight. My father turned as well. His weighty stare made the man step backward, but it wasn't enough to make him apologize. The man straightened his tunic and raised his eyes to me and Da.

"You know what you are. Don't act like it's my fault," he said. Da continued to stare for a moment, then his glance flickered to me. I saw it. The shame.

My ears burned. I pushed between them and ran. The image of the girl burning brightly in my mind. Her image chased me as I hurtled down the path to our cabin at the edge of camp.

Eusebia glowed from sunup to sundown. Instead of resenting her, like I did the others, her light drew me to her. She had the lightest hair of any Lightwalker I'd ever seen, and she was fierce enough with a knife that I wondered if she might be able to land a hit even on me.

Eusebia was a golden child. She was favored by the camp elders and peers alike, because her light production was so high.

It was more than that though. She was a good-hearted girl, always ready with a laugh. She was willing to do whatever work was set before her, no matter how base it might be. And when it came to the fighting that we were all required to learn, she was willing to pull her tawny hair back and do that work as well. I was a sunken ship before I ever even spoke to her.

I was on the outside of that circle of light. The elders acknowledged me, but only in the barest of ways. I was always given the lowest of chores, and there were plenty in camp who wouldn't even speak to me. It churned my guts, but what could I do? I was only a boy.

I'd given up my hope of running away from my father. There was nowhere for me to go. Without another Lightwalker willing to share with me, I'd be dead within a day. Roderic had made it clear that I wasn't welcome to come live with him and Heva. The healer tents even sent me home after a few days, always making room for those who were really injured. Where else could I go?

Da hadn't grown fonder or friendlier since Heva had left. Now that I knew he was taking light from healers, I watched the tent so we would not appear there at the same time. We barely spoke to each other, moving in loose circles around each other. I went to sleep late and rose early, anything to avoid the suffocating air between us.

As often as I could, I trained. I was good at all the woodcrafts, and I found that I preferred to be in the woods than in a cabin. If only I could get enough light to survive, I would disappear into the forest without a backward glance.

Stay. The Voice still spoke to me, though not as often as when I was younger. I struggled against the Voice now. It was always telling me to stay with my people, with my Da. The Voice had never led me wrong before, so I stayed.

I walked through camp, avoiding the gazes of the others.

Stay, The Voice pleaded. I ignored it when women pulled their children back from me.

Stay, The Voice continued. I looked away when men twice my age growled at me, or told me to "get!" like a dog.

Stay.

I climbed the abandoned paths that led to the old mine west of camp. It had long ago given up the last of its iron ore, and had since been closed. Now the miners went to the north of camp and worked a new vein. No one came here any more, so I had made it my refuge.

There was a waterfall that dried up in winter. Now I stood at its peak, looking down at the long fall to the basin of water that lingered year-round. It would be no deeper than a handspan now. It wouldn't be enough to break my fall. I looked at the bare edge, my toe extending past it into open air. There was nothing, absolutely nothing, to stop me from stepping forward and ending it all.

Stay. Please.

"Please?" I asked, exasperated. "How can you ask this of me? You know what my life is like. There's not a soul here that wants me. It would be better for everyone if I disappeared and you know it!"

Instead of answering, there was silence. I was frustrated, and there were tears blurring my vision. I wiped them away, embarrassed that they were there. What was there even to grieve, other than the injustice of it all? A life wasted? Not much of one.

"I can't keep on like this," I said. "I won't make it another year, another month, at this rate. I must have a reason to keep going, or I swear I'll come up here and no amount of your pleases will keep me from jumping."

Instead of answering with words, I looked out at the blue sky and saw Eusebia. It was my own memory of her, smiling and glowing brightly, the way she'd looked the very first time I'd seen her.

A sob welled up in my throat, and I choked it down. Of all the things to show me!

I picked up a rock and threw it as hard as I could, knowing it could never touch the vision in the sky.

"That was low, even for you," I said to The Voice. "She probably doesn't even know my name."

Then I looked up, and the vision had changed. Now it showed Heva, her three children at her side, and her belly swelling with another. Helm and Osuin were looking up at her and she was explaining how I'd died to them. There were tears on her cheeks. Her hand went to her stomach, and her face clenched in pain.

My stomach churned, and I sat down, legs dangling over the edge.

"That can't be true," I said, watching the image dissipate like a cloud broken apart by the wind. "It can't be."

It will be if you give up now.

"I don't know if I believe you this time," I said. It was true. The Voice had never lied to me before, but telling me the future? That was a far stretch.

The Voice didn't defend itself, didn't respond at all. But I knew it was still there, hovering over me like a heat around a fire.

"And after Heva has her next baby? What's to stop me then?" I asked. I doubted I'd feel much better about my life, even if Heva had twenty babies.

There are people in your future who will need you. You're going to want to be around to help them, boy.

I laughed then. "You're saying if I die here, I'll regret it? I'll be *dead!* How would that work?"

The Voice didn't answer, but the moment had passed. The sun traveled its way across the sky, and when it started to slide back toward the edge of the world, I went home. I'd stay around long enough for Heva's baby to be born. On this day, I could promise no more.

Part Two

Chapter Four

Someone is coming.

I sat bolt upright, listening. I was in a tree, lounging, waiting for the healer tent to empty out a little more. I could sneak in just before long shadows and get enough to survive the night.

It was a few seconds of waiting before I heard it. Footsteps. I scrambled down the tree trunk and waited. The Voice hadn't sounded alarmed, so neither was I.

Before long, Heva appeared. She stopped, and we stared at each other for a moment.

How long had it been since we'd spoken last? Could it have been as long as a full season? Surely not. I saw the boys in the meadow, training, all the time. I realized I hadn't seen my own sister in too long though.

She was different now. Her hair wasn't as shiny as I remembered, and her body had changed since her multiple pregnancies. She still had a wariness in her eyes, and I understood too well what that meant. I had it in mine, as well.

31

"Gast." She was the only one who called me that, and a part of me felt like a child upon hearing it.

"Heva," I answered, still waiting. I no longer ran to her to hug her waist. At eighteen, I towered over her in height. It was still strange to look down at her, instead of up.

"Do you need light?" she asked, and I pulled my arms back, a silent refusal. I didn't want Roderic's light. I didn't want his charity.

"I'm fine," I said tersely. "What do you want?"

Heva didn't meet my eyes. She reached into the pouch dangling from her shoulder.

"I brought you something, brother," she said. I frowned. It had been a long time since she'd brought me anything, even bread. A house full of five children kept her far too occupied to keep tending to me and Da.

I stepped closer, and tugged my tunic back into place. Whatever she had come to say, I supposed I could walk her home after. There would still be time to gather up light from a healer.

"Here." She held a knife in a leather sheath out to me.

"What's this?" I asked. I had plenty of knives. Da was a knifemaker and it was the one interest we shared.

"Gast," she said, finally meeting my eyes. "You're eighteen. You know what happens then."

My eyes widened.

"You think I'm going to marry?" I asked, shocked.

"I think that no matter what happens," she said, heading off the protests that were about to come. "You are going to have to find a kind of family for yourself. Whether it's a family you create with a woman, or whether it's one you find, you can't keep going on alone. Lightwalkers aren't meant to be alone, little brother."

I met her eyes, but didn't take the knife. I knew she hadn't the time to make it herself. She hadn't been at her knifemaking in more than a year. Did she buy it? With Roderic's money? No, thank you.

With a sigh, she lowered her hand.

"Gast, you can't go on with so much anger," she said softly.

"Can't I?" I asked. The Voice, I knew, agreed with my sister. But she didn't need to know that. The anger was the only thing that kept me going. I lived on it, ate it like bread and slept with it like a lover.

"I doubt I'll be allowed to marry, Heva."

"They have to give you a light partner," she said.

"Yes, but I could refuse one."

"You wouldn't!" she gasped. I knew her response was normal. No one refused a light partner. It was suicide. But I'd been living off of light borrowed from healer tents for years. I didn't want to attach myself to a single Lightwalker, and have to face the pity in their eyes day after day. I couldn't.

"I can and I will," I said. Heva searched my eyes, and I could see the fear brimming in hers. She was afraid for me. I wondered what she'd see reflected in mine?

"I haven't died yet, sister," I said.

"I'm not sure you're really alive, either," she answered.

I thought, ridiculously, about Eusebia. She had smiled at me. I'm sure it was just a passing thing. She smiled at everyone. I had only happened to be in her line of sight. But it had felt like I'd been chosen by the very sun, for that small moment.

"I don't think I'll be allowed much more than the life I have," I said. But I couldn't bear the fear in my sister's eyes. So I smiled down at her, a shrug on my shoulders. "Don't worry, Heva. I'll be okay."

"Take it anyway," Heva said, shoving the knife my way. "One day, you may want to call someone family. When you do, give this to them. It's a worthy gift. The handle is deer antler, and I took down the animal myself."

I looked at the knife pressed against my chest, and gathered it in my hands. Pulling the knife out of the leather sheath, I saw that it was smaller. It was meant for a woman's hand. Or maybe a child's.

I looked back at Heva, but she was already turning away. Did she really think I'd ever have a chance to pass this on to either? I realized then that was why her light had felt different than my father's.

She still had hope.

Chapter Five

The council decided as I'd predicted. No marriage. No family. I would be assigned a light partner, and expected to start participating in runs.

Well, that was fine by me. The longer the run, the better. I'd hedged about having a light partner. I decided I'd wait to see who I was assigned to, at least. Maybe there was still some hope left in me, too. I had no hope of a family of my own, but maybe I could still manage to steal away a brother.

My rebel heart held a tenuous thread of hope that I'd be assigned to Eusebia. She had enough light to spare. I knew it was a fool's hope. The council almost never paired unwed men and women together.

The council gave me my first run assignment and my light partner in the same meeting. We were leaving in the morning, at first light. My partner was to be a boy a year older than me named Colias.

I went home for what might be the last time. In the morning, I'd leave for a run and my adult life in Iron Camp would begin. Or I'd die on the trail. Either way, my childhood was over.

Da was waiting in the house, but he didn't say anything when I crossed the threshold. There were a couple of fresh loaves of bread on the table, so I knew Heva must have come by.

She must be worried about me. Heva hadn't brought bread in months.

"Were you called up for service?" Da asked. He was squatting in front of the fireplace, watching the flames dance.

"Yes."

"When do you leave?" he asked.

"First thing in the morning," I said. My back was to him, so he couldn't see my frown. We rarely spoke and he hadn't questioned me about my whereabouts since I was a kid. Even then, it had been more for Heva's sake than mine.

"Good," he said. "That's good."

I turned to look at him. He still had his back to me.

"My son. A runner."

I held my breath. Da cleared his throat, looked back at me for a brief glance.

"Going to step out for a moment. Get yourself some rest. You'll need it out there."

"Yes, sir," I said, my brow still creased. I watched him stand and take long strides toward the front door. There, he paused.

"Cunigast," he said.

"Yes?"

"You're a better man than I am. Don't let them take that from you."

I had no words for that. Silently, I watched my father leave the house. The exchange was so strange, it circled my head for the rest of the evening. I tucked myself into bed early, but it was a long time before I slept.

The next morning, I found my father's talisman and the handkerchief my mother had embroidered for him under a rock on the porch rail. There was a slim piece of paper. It read, *Forgive me.*

I picked up the talisman that bore his name, and my own as nearest kin. It took a full minute for me to understand.

My father had lightburst. He was dead, by his own device. It was a Lightwalker suicide, letting out all of your light at once. There would be nothing left of him besides this, and maybe a pile of clothing in the forest.

I sucked in a breath. Gods Above! I was supposed to leave this very morning! Who should I tell? What should I do?

Tears slipped down my cheeks, shocking me completely.

My father was dead.

Breathe.

I released the breath I'd been holding and drew in another. *Gods Above! Gods Above!*

Breathe, Cunigast.

I could do little else for a while. It took everything in me to clear my eyes, to still my shaking hands. A glance at the sky told me I had little time before I was expected by my team.

Go find Heva.

Heva! How on the land was I going to tell her? I looked at the talisman dangling in my hand, and knew I wouldn't have to say a word.

I gathered up the handkerchief and the note alongside the talisman and took off running. Heva, at the very least, would know what to do. Wouldn't she? I hoped so, because my mind was reeling.

In a matter of moments, I was pounding on her door.

"Heva!" I shouted. "I need you!"

Roderic answered, his face a thundercloud.

I don't have time for you!

"Heva!" I shouted again, right over his shoulder.

Heva materialized in a moment.

"Nevermind him," she said, sparing a moment to glare a warning over her shoulder. "What is it?"

I held out my hands.

Heva gasped, her hands going to her throat.

"Gods Above! He didn't!"

"He did."

Our eyes met for a frantic moment. She was already crying. I looked away. I wouldn't cry in front of Roderic. I *would not.*

"What do we do, Heva?" I asked. "I'm due at the stables in less than a turning to leave on my first run. There isn't time. There isn't-" my voice cracked. I stopped, choking back all the feelings brimming inside of me.

Heva was already nodding. She turned to her husband.

"Roderic, go get an elder. Any elder. Wake them up if you have to!" she said. "Run!"

He was out the door, though it was clear he didn't agree with her.

"Go home and pack up for your run," Heva said. "I'll handle everything."

"The vigil!"

"I'll handle everything." Our eyes met again. Hers was filled with iron this time.

When a Lightwalker died, a brazier was lit in the center of the camp square. The usual custom was for the closest kin to stand vigil until the light burned out. It sometimes took days. Heva couldn't stay awake for that long.

"I'll go pack, but I doubt they'll let me go now," I answered thickly. I couldn't decide how to feel about it. Heva was already shoving me out the door though.

"He lightburst, Heva. Our father," I said, standing on her steps. I was a ship at sea with no sail.

"I know, Cunigast. But there's nothing we can do about it now."

It was a taboo in Lightwalker culture, to lightburst. Taking your own life was seen as a waste of light. That light could have been used to kill a breacher, after all. But my father hadn't been on a run in memory. What had he really wasted?

I thought of the handkerchief he'd been carrying for almost two decades and my throat constricted. Gods Above! I didn't know how he'd lasted this long!

But frustration was building right along with my grief. Heva and I would be children of a lightburster from now on. It was a mark against us when we couldn't bear any more. Low light producing, motherless...now our father had failed us again by killing himself. No wonder why his final note had been to ask forgiveness. There was a lot to forgive.

A knife of pain slipped between my ribs, and I gasped as if I'd been truly stabbed. *My father is dead! My father!*

We had never been close. Maybe that was what hurt the most. I'd shared a cabin with him my entire life and apparently he'd been waiting for the moment I'd become old enough to stand on my own to kill himself. If it had been so important, why couldn't he have bothered to *speak* to me in the interim?

I stumbled into our cabin and the emptiness pressed against me like an oppressive ghost. His absence filled the place. I couldn't breathe. There was no air in that place.

I slammed my gear into my pack and threw myself onto the porch with the force of a lightning strike, sick at heart.

I can't live here anymore! I swear, I'll go mad!

I was relieved from my thoughts by Heva striding down the path, her steps long and quick. An elder was coming close on her heels, a man older than my father, his grey hair pulled into a long tail behind him that swung with his gait.

"Cunigast!" Heva called. She must have seen the terrible blankness on my face. Or terrible panic. I wasn't sure which.

"I'm here," I said, desperate to catch my breath.

"Young man," the elder called, catching up slower. "Young man, your run has been postponed."

I deflated. "They are leaving without me?"

"No," he said, with a frown. "The numbers wouldn't be balanced. The others will wait."

A relief, if a small one.

"Once you've held vigil for your father, you'll go on your run as planned. It's a delay of a few days. The other elders agree. You and your sister should have a few days to attend to this. It's only right."

I was nodding my head, but inwardly, I cringed. I would be expected to sleep in that cavernous house alone tonight. I couldn't breathe in there, how would I *sleep* in there? They were likely to find me dead in the morning.

Heva must have seen the panic.

"I'll stay with you, brother."

"What will Roderic have to say about that?" I asked, frowning.

"You're my brother. He will live," she answered easily enough. The elder was watching the exchange with mild interest.

"Both of you should come up to the council lodge. We'll speak to you about what arrangements must be made."

"Arrangements?" I asked. As far as I knew, holding the vigil in the square was the only arrangement that needed making. Heva and I could go light it right now, if we wanted. In fact, I did want to. The sooner I could get this over with, the better.

"Young man, there are other concerns to attend to. Who will get his home? Who will take over his work? I know he wasn't a runner, but he got up and contributed to this camp every day. Someone will have to pick up the slack."

"He was a knifemaker," Heva said, her voice as sharp as her knives. "I always planned to take over for him. I could do so now."

"My child, you are expected to stay home with your children, not make knives."

"As I am not pregnant currently," Heva answered through gritted teeth. "I doubt it will hurt me to make a few knives now."

The man blinked at her, missing her affront entirely.

"It must be discussed, either way." He turned and began walking away. Heva and I trailed behind.

"You're expected to stay home with your children!" I mimicked the old man ahead of us.

"That is what they'd prefer," she answered. She sounded as cold as ice and I knew she was angry.

"What are you going to do?" I asked.

"Don't worry about me, Cunigast. I can take care of myself."

I snorted. As if there'd been any doubt about that.

"What will you do, Cunigast?" she asked.

"I guess we'll find out if I can take care of myself."

She stopped on the path.

"Promise me something, Cunigast," she said seriously, turning to face me. "Promise me that you won't do this. What Da did. Promise me you'll never..."

Her voice trailed off, but I couldn't fill the silence that followed. Promise to never lightburst? Well, I'd stood atop the cliff a handful of times over the years and contemplated that long, final step. But I'd never thought about lightbursting.

If I was honest, I was afraid to learn that I didn't even have enough light to kill myself. Still, Heva was looking at me with wide eyes verging on panic.

"I promise, Heva." I said, sincerely hoping I meant it.

Chapter Six

Heva and I lit the brazier full of oil for our father. It was toward evening, and we were alone in the square.

It wasn't right. A man had died and there was no one to stand vigil for him except his own two children. He'd been born here, lived his life here. Every day he got up and worked near the smithy. Where were his friends? The people he worked alongside? Gods Above, half the village was carrying a knife he'd made with his own hands! Could none of them be bothered to watch the brazier be lit in his honor?

I gritted my teeth and held my sister's hand. Roderic had offered to come, but Heva had sent him home. I was glad. I didn't want him there.

I knew why we were alone. It was his manner of death. It was a dishonor to lightburst. No one would say a word to our faces, but this was the camp's silent protest. They wouldn't stand vigil for a man who'd ended his own light.

Gods Above I hate them all!

Try to forgive them, Cunigast.

I'm standing alone with my sister at my father's vigil, and you ask me to forgive them? What do I owe any of them? What have any of them ever done for me to earn my forgiveness?

You don't forgive them for them. You do it for yourself, child.

I closed my mind to The Voice. I could not hear it and stay sane. Not tonight.

The brazier was alight for three days. Heva and I took turns after the first night. I slept in the healer's tents. They assumed it was grief. Truthfully I couldn't face that empty cabin, though it was now mine alone. The elders had decided it the same day we lit the brazier for him.

A full day after the light went out, my run was set to start. I still had not met my new partner, Colias. I supposed he wasn't concerned with sharing light with me until our official meeting on our first run. It was just as well. I'd been grouchy as a bear since waking to find my father's talisman on the porch rail.

I shouldered my pack of gear and headed for the horse stables. I wondered what sort of fellow this Colias would be. I didn't remember him from our training as children, but he was a year older than me, and likely put into different training groups.

I met him at the gate. It was clear from the first moment that he was not happy to have me as his light partner. The look that glossed over me as I led my horse to the gate was enough to set the anger simmering in my veins.

Keep going. The Voice was prodding me. I wanted to run away right then. I wanted to reject this man before he could reject me. I wanted to turn back to the council and refuse all of it. Partner, run, place in the community, all of it.

With lead feet, I kept moving forward. The Voice had not lied to me yet, so I kept going.

Colias turned, leaning against his horse and nodded at me.

"So we're to be light partners," he said. The disdain was heavy. I couldn't say I felt much better about it.

"Yes, that's what they tell me."

"I almost never need light given. I have to share extra," he said. It was a brag and a sneer and slight to me all in one. I just nodded.

"I can take whatever you have to share," I said. The words ate at my pride.

Colias opened his mouth to speak more, but instead his focus went over my shoulder. I turned, and my mouth went dry.

Eusebia was walking down the path, leading her horse. Another girl was at her side, and the two of them were laughing.

What was she doing here? Was she going on the same run?

No. Please, no.

But it was soon clear that she was. I thought I'd die right where I stood.

"Good morning, boys," she said, and went back to talking with her friend. The two girls were checking their tack, checking their saddlebags, making sure there weren't any last minute items they needed to take.

Eusebia pulled a bandana from her pocket and began tying it around her neck. I fingered the bandana in my own pocket, knowing I'd have to do the same. Every Lightwalker had one, and wore them any time they left camp. A stripe was added for every breacher kill.

Blank. My bandana was totally blank.

For this, at least, my shame was irrational. I hadn't gone on any runs, so there had been no opportunity to take down a breacher. And the three people standing closest to me were just as young and inexperienced. We all had blank bandanas.

Mine won't be blank for long. Not if I can help it.

It was a vow I'd been making to myself for years. I'd be the best at *everything*, that included taking down breachers. I just had to find one.

Chapter Seven

The run turned out to be a slow death for me. Eusebia was everywhere, always at the periphery of my consciousness and rarely out of my line of sight. I didn't speak to her, and resisted looking at her as much as I could. But I always knew exactly where she was, and spent hours stiff in the saddle, tense with the desire to be in her circle of light.

Eusebia was a Lightwalker woman through and through. She was intense about fighting and scouting, fierce with a knife and a natural born horsewoman. But in the camp, she laughed freely with the others, whispered with the women and teased the men.

Well, other men. Somehow I wasn't included in any teasing or even casual conversation. Every time her gaze swung in my direction, my heart pounded in my ears and I found a reason to walk away.

Colias, if he noticed, said nothing. In fact, he spoke almost as little as Eusebia did to me. There were four of us on our first run, and another two who were seasoned Lightwalker runners. Tor, a fierce man in his middle years with a neck as thick as a tree trunk led our group. His wife,

Lasha was in second command, and she was nearly as aggressive as her husband, though packaged in a smaller body. I wouldn't have wished to fight either, though I'd taken down men just as large. Lasha was tricky, and just as likely to hurt you as clap your shoulder and congratulate you.

Colias and I were forced to share space often, being the two youngest males. Being light partners meant Colias shared with me twice a day. I felt good. I'd never been so healthy and strong, having always had to beg the dregs of light from healers at the end of long work days. Colias was pumping me full of light that set my veins on fire. I could run faster, jump higher, and fight for days. Maybe having a light partner who hated me would be a fair enough trade to keep feeling like this.

At night, I wondered what it would be like to lightshare with Eusebia. Heva's light had been stringent, but tinged with hope. Da's felt like just as much darkness fed into me as light. The healers in the tents tended to feel like a trickle, a precious hoarded commodity. They doled out only enough to keep me alive for another day. They always needed extra on board in case someone truly injured arrived. Colias's light felt like sunshine at the hottest part of the day, pressing down on me like it was a threat. I felt flattened under it, until I could run some of the edge off.

What would Eusebia's light feel like? I couldn't decide on a word other than *good*.

"Cunigast!" Tor snapped. I had been in my head again. *Gathering wool,* Heva called it.

I surged forward on my horse, passing Colias and Eusebia to reach him. As I drew abreast, he held up a hand.

"Scout ahead, boy," Tor said, jerking his head down the trail. "Be sharp. Think there's something going on up there."

I'd already proven myself to be a capable scout to Tor. This wasn't an unusual request on the face of it. I'd long begun to suspect that I was also the most expendable of the group as well.

"On horse?" I asked. If he suspected something, he was likely right. The old runner was rarely wrong about these things.

"Treetops, if you can manage it," he answered. I showed all of my teeth, letting him know what I thought of that.

Instead of answering, I tossed a long line from my horse to Colias, and stood in the saddle. Soon enough a tree branch passed low enough, and I latched on. It was a matter of seconds to pull myself up and disappear into the treetops.

Feet as sure as a squirrel's, I crossed from tree to tree at their thickest points, and soon had skipped ahead enough that I could no longer see our little huddle of Lightwalkers.

Tor was right. A stone's throw ahead there was a group of downlanders on the path. I could see the bear traps dangling from horse haunches.

Poachers.

I knew this would end in a fight, but I wasn't worried. I turned to report back to Tor.

Wait.

The men parted, and between horses, I could see a bundle of cloth and hair shivering there.

A woman. Girl, more like.

The tallest of the men, a broad-shouldered man with a thick paunch, leaned over her, and she cringed away. She was crying, and holding her clothes in place like they'd fall off if she let go. There was a bruise on her cheek.

A rushing sound like wind filled my ears until it shut down all other senses.

I should go back for the others. I should report back to Tor.

The man reached for the girl, jerking her forward so hard that her head snapped back painfully. She whimpered, and the man crushed her against himself. The other men shuffled closer, and the air grew thick.

Without thought, I leapt forward, knife already drawn and moving. A blade sunk into the neck of the big man before the others knew I was among them.

But among them, I was.

Another knife filled my empty hand, and I set about my task. Quick cuts and hard hits had them running or sprawled at my feet. It was over in moments. I stood there, tracking the ones who had run. They fled in the opposite direction of my group.

Turning, I saw the girl. She looked at me with wide eyes, still trembling from head to toe. I must have looked terrifying. Slowly, I sheathed my knives, wiped my hands against my deer hide shirt and held them up and open.

"Easy, girl," I said softly. "I'm not going to hurt you."

Instead of answering, she slumped forward. Instinctively, I caught her. She had fainted.

Unsure what else to do, I hoisted her up in front of me on one of the horses, and rode back to the others.

Tor and Lasha had hidden the others in the brush, obviously waiting to learn what had happened to their scout. I whistled once, long and low, imitating an upland bird. Tor's head appeared, followed closely by the others.

"Gods Above! What have you done, boy?" Lasha called.

Lasha rushed forward to take the girl. I was glad to give her over to the women. I gave the full report to Tor, who looked angrier and angrier with every word.

"Motherless, white-bellied, sons of ..." his voice trailed off, his eyes going distant over my shoulder. "I suppose we have a mess to clean up then. Come on," he said, calling over his shoulder to Colias. "Let the women tend to the girl. We'll deal with this."

The "mess" hadn't grown prettier in my absence. There were three men dead on the ground, and five live horses, not including the one I'd ridden back. The biggest one still had my knife in his neck.

Colias whistled, then raised an eyebrow at me, reevaluating me. I straightened. Would this change the disdain in his voice when he had to lightshare?

"Clean deaths," Tor said. It was a compliment from the old runner and I took it to heart.

Long hours later, the three men were buried. We'd stripped the horses of their hunting tack, and set them loose. Some other camp could collect them, if they wished. We had no need for them.

"Bear traps," Tor hissed, followed by more cursing. I nodded. Lightwalkers didn't take poaching lightly. We weren't yet out of Lightwalker territory, having chosen to skirt through the highest regions to the far west, just under the lip of the mountains. Tor planned to bring us downland in a few days, cutting across the southern shore until we reached Lux. There were no settlements here, aside from the scattering of Lightwalker cabins. No downlander should have been here.

It did beg a question though.

"Where on the land did they get the girl?" Colias asked, sharing my thoughts. I looked to Tor for an answer.

"Three days due east will land you at a small downlander settlement. From the looks of her, she's already been badly used. Maybe they picked her up there," Tor said with a shrug. The idea of that girl being in such rough company for three days churned my guts.

Why couldn't I have found her sooner?

Imagine if you hadn't waited? The thought stopped me in my tracks. I had been about to leave! The Voice had asked me to wait, and moments later, I'd seen her.

Thank you for keeping me there longer, I answered The Voice, my hand curling tightly into a fist. The idea that I might have walked away and left her there...

I turned aside and retched. Tor smacked my back hard.

"Better out than in, boy. Get it out before you have to look at the girl again."

Was he speaking from experience? I shuddered at the thought.

Moments later, I had recovered. My stomach was still watery, but there was no trace of the horror on my face. It was a good thing, too. When the three of us stepped into the circle of light from the campfire, the girl screamed.

"Shh, it's only Cunigast," Eusebia said, rubbing the girl's back. "He saved you, remember? He won't hurt you. None of them will."

I was never so glad when dinner was done and I could roll myself up in a bedroll and sleep. But that girl's wide eyes haunted me long after I closed my own.

Chapter Eight

We turned eastward two days later, the girl in tow on the one horse we hadn't turned loose. She was silent and frightened, wincing any time one of the men drew closer than a stone's throw. Eusebia never left her side, whispering who-knows-what in her ear. They took furtive looks at me, and I dutifully ignored them, though my ears burned.

"Would you quit that?" Colias growled at me, later in the evening. We were rubbing down the horses while the others made dinner.

"Quit what?" I asked, straightening to look at him over Lasha's horse.

"That girl keeps looking at you because you're the one who rescued her. But she's a downlander, and little more than a child. Your ears turn red every time she looks at you," Colias growled, narrowing his eyes at me as if I'd made a pass at the girl.

I balled my fists, resisting the urge to hit him.

"I don't give two ticks about that little girl!" I answered, growling right back.

"Then what's with the blushing, eh?" he challenged.

I opened my mouth and then snapped it back shut.

"That's what I thought," he smirked, and started to walk away.

"It's not her," I said softly as he passed.

Which was worse? Him thinking I hankered after a downlander girl, or knowing that I was dying with want of Eusebia?

"What does that mean?" Colias asked. He blinked his big dumb eyes at me, and I knew I'd have to say it, the thing I hadn't dared speak even to myself.

"It's not the girl," I whispered. "It's Eusebia."

Colias's eyes widened, and he stepped back as if I'd slapped him.

"Eusebia!" he said, his voice rising. I slapped a hand over his mouth and glanced behind him. No one was there, thank the Gods Above!

"Shut it!" I whispered, moving my hand away.

"You're a fool if you think-"

"I know," I interrupted. "Don't you think that I, of all people, know it's a fool's chance? Worse than that, it's no chance at all."

My hands were curled into tight fists, my chest aching. I felt the same as when Heva told me she'd been taking light from healers just to keep me going.

"I know what I am, Colias. I won't get a wife or a family of my own. I will be lucky to die on a run taking down a breacher." I met his eyes, and was surprised to find surprise. Whatever he'd expected from this conversation, this wasn't it. "You don't have to worry about me doing anything foolish, Colias. I know my place."

I was shaking, I was so angry. I started to walk away, shadow creatures be blighted.

I was shocked, then, when Colias's hand landed hard on my shoulder, pinning me in place. Light began trickling into my skin where his fingers dug into my shoulder. Instead of the breath-stealing heaviness that his light usually gave me, this time it felt light as air and bright as a river. It trickled down into my bones until I felt as if I might float away.

Eyes as wide as horseshoes, I looked at him.

He just let go and walked away.

Chapter Nine

Three days later, we left the downlander girl with a Church of Othniel in a little village hardly large enough to support one. We handed over the bear traps and the tack from the horses.

"I'd suggest you melt those traps down for nails, priest," Tor grunted. "Maybe sell the tack to get the girl a fresh start."

The white-robed man had taken her in without question, and asked if we needed fodder for our horses.

This was my first encounter with a priest of Othniel, and I watched the man with curiosity. He had hair that was thinning, but not yet white and a squinty look that I guessed meant he was nearsighted. He smiled easily at us, but didn't invite us in.

What did the Gods Above make of these priests? They followed Othniel, a Lightwalker from some three hundred and fifty years ago who'd descended the mountain and made a splash amongst the downlanders. As far as any of us could tell, they didn't know that Othniel was just a Lightwalker. As far as I could tell, they didn't care.

We turned our horses for the forest, and continued on our way, avoiding the little settlements that began dotting the landscape.

"What do they do out here?" I asked, riding alongside Lasha. She was a small woman, and she rode a small horse. It made these conversations a tad awkward. I felt like I was towering over her, and I knew from experience that she would bite if provoked.

"What do you think, kid?" she asked, huffing. "They live off the land like anyone else does."

"Doing what? They don't have access to the mountains like we do," I said, looking around the forest surrounding us. "And they aren't allowed to collect too much of the timber."

"They hunt, they farm where they can, they fish the river," Lasha said, shrugging. "They survive."

"Doesn't sound like much of a life," I said honestly.

"The smart ones go further downland," she answered. "The rest struggle on."

I wondered about that girl we'd just dropped off. It felt like a tragedy to rescue her, for her to starve the next winter.

Injustice curled in my stomach and wouldn't be dislodged, no matter the miles that separated us.

Behind me, Eusebia and her light partner, Naomi, were drawing closer.

"There's a river nearby!" Eusebia said, smiling. She wasn't asking, so she must have seen it through the trees. She always had a good eye.

"Aye," Lasha answered. "What of it?"

"Can we go swimming?" Eusebia asked, practically bouncing in the saddle. Beside her, Naomi was just as excited.

"Swimming? The water will be freezing!" Lasha answered.

"Surely no colder than the rivers back home!" Eusebia exclaimed, undaunted. I saw her ploy for what it was. "I've seen you swim back home."

"Of course it's not *colder* than back home, but it's plenty cold enough!"

"It's not too cold for me."

"Hmph!" Lasha put her heels to her little horse and surged forward, leaving the three of us. I looked between Naomi and Eusebia, expecting them to draw away from me.

Instead, they both rode forward until they were abreast with my horse, one on each side.

I tugged at my hair, wondering if my ears were as red as Colias had accused.

"You're a good swimmer, Cunigast," Eusebia said happily, as if we were old friends. That was how she talked to everyone, though. "Will you go swimming with us?"

"I don't think Lasha is going to let us," I answered, looking ahead to where Lasha was riding alongside her husband. They were talking about something, and both of her hands were waving around.

"You'll see," Eusebia said. "She will do it just to prove the water isn't too cold for her. She's terribly competitive, you know."

I did know, but it seemed unkind to play that against the woman. I eyed Eusebia for a moment. Had I misjudged her?

"Oh don't look so fishy at me, Gast!" she said, a smile turning up the corners of her mouth.

I stopped breathing. No one had called me that, except Heva.

"Eusebia!" Naomi gasped. "Don't tease Cunigast!"

"He doesn't mind," Eusebia said, leaning forward to look at her friend. Then she smiled up at me. "You don't, do you?"

I shook my head, not trusting myself to breath.

"So you'll come with us, won't you?" she asked again.

"If Tor doesn't give me another job, I'll go swimming."

"The water isn't too cold for you, either," she said with a smile. Was she teasing me? Goading me? I had no idea. But if she asked me to bathe in the coldest river on the land, I'd jump in head first.

I'm an idiot.

Fortunately, The Voice didn't bother to answer that.

Chapter Ten

Three hours later, we were all standing at the edge of a quiet river that was the color of stone. Eusebia stood on one side of me, and Colias on the other.

"Let's all jump in together!" Eusebia said jittering up and down on the balls of her feet. There was a challenge in her voice, and I didn't miss it. On her other side, Naomi groaned. Apparently, she'd heard it too.

"I don't know that I want to *jump* in, Eusebia," Naomi pouted. She was far less competitive than Eusebia.

"It's better this way, and you know it," Eusebia said. "Better to get in all at once than waste time tip-toeing about it."

"Maybe I like tip-toeing!" Naomi pouted again.

"I can wait and go in with you, Naomi," Colias said, surprising me to my toes. Was he sweet on her? I hadn't noticed. "If you want."

"Cunigast will jump in with me, won't you?" Eusebia said, turning to look up at me. Those honey-colored eyes pierced me through. I just nodded.

She smiled, her cheeks full of color. Then she grabbed my hand and jumped.

We were on a short ledge, and I barely had time to suck in a breath before we plunged into the water, Eusebia's hand still caught in mine.

The water was icy cold, chilling my veins, and clear as glass. I opened my eyes to see Eusebia suspended in the water next to me. She swam closer, our fingers tangled together, and pressed her lips to mine. Then she put a finger to her lips and surged upward for air.

Mind reeling, I followed. I broke out of the water like a fish to find the world turned upside down.

Had Eusebia just kissed me? Surely, I'd imagined the whole thing. But when I looked over at her, she was smiling and her cheeks were bright red.

"The water's fine!" She shouted up to Naomi and Colias on the ledge. "Jump in!"

But Naomi was shaking her head. She started back down the path to where the water met the shore at a softer angle. Colias trailed behind her.

I was treading water, waiting for the world to make sense again. Water splashed into my face, and I turned. Eusebia had splashed me.

Gods Above was she *flirting* with me? My eyes widened.

For the moment, we were alone. Lasha and Tor were already in the water farther down, being unforgivably neglectful of their charges. Colias and Naomi were out of sight. Eusebia swam closer.

"I hope I didn't surprise you too badly," she said, still smiling.

Too badly? I didn't think I'd ever recover. But I shook my head.

"You don't talk much, do you?"

I stared at her some more. My arms were treading water madly, but I'd drown before I broke off this one tenuous moment.

"What did you want me to say?" I asked. She leaned back, floating for a moment on her back, and laughed.

"Anything at all, Gast," she said. "You can say anything you like to me."

"I doubt that's true." I sounded gruff to my own ears.

"I see you staring at me, you know," she said. Her eyes were closed, and she was floating as peacefully as a star in the sky.

I didn't bother with floating. There was no way I'd be able to relax enough to do it right now. The blood was beating in my ears again, and I couldn't think of a thing to say. There was no denying it.

"I don't mean to," I said.

"Yes, you do," she said, opening her eyes. Colias and Naomi would be back any moment. Where were they anyway?

"I don't mean to bother you," I said more truthfully.

"It doesn't bother me," she answered. "I just wish you would talk to me instead."

There was no hope that I wasn't blushing now. I sank down in the water, hoping to hide some of it under the unhelpfully clear water.

"Don't go." She reached out, placed her hands to my chest, and drew herself into the circle of my arms. I floundered, kicking hard to keep afloat. She wrapped her arms around me and kicked, too. Together, we floated in the water, suspended in time and space for an aching moment.

"I meant what I said, Cunigast," she said. There were droplets of water in her eyelashes. "You can say anything at all to me."

Then she let go and swam away.

I blinked. Naomi and Colias were swimming toward us, a wake of splashing water trailing them. Eusebia had seen them before I had.

I let myself sink down into the icy cold water, and wondered when I resurfaced if the world would ever look the same again.

Chapter Eleven

It didn't. The rest of the trip was filled with meaningful stares over campfires and stolen moments alone. If no one was close enough to see, she would draw closer and thread her fingers through mine. If Naomi drew far enough ahead and Colias drew far enough behind, she would talk to me in whispers on the trail.

"I saw you take down that deer, Cunigast," she would say. Or, "I wish I could climb to the treetops with you, Cunigast."

They were silly things, mostly meaningless. The words filled me up like sunshine. There were the smallest of touches, but no more stolen kisses like the one underwater. I lay awake at night, thinking about that too-brief moment.

What were we doing? There was no way the council would let me marry her. I knew it, and surely she must as well. So what did that make this? A little adventure before she was forced to marry? A fling? There were lines that could never be crossed, chastity being a highly valued commodity for both Lightwalker men and women. But these little touches between fingers and mouths?

I surely would take whatever I could, knowing full well that that little kiss in the river might be the only one I ever got for the rest of my life. But I also knew it would never be enough.

I had to wonder, could a man die from longing? Was this filling the hole left by my loneliness or making it worse? It already hurt. But I could deny her nothing.

"Gast!"

I turned my head. It was nighttime, and I was lying awake in my bedroll. Eusebia was awake in hers. Around us, everyone else was asleep. She jerked her head to one side, and started rising, disappearing on quiet feet into the darkness.

I rose and followed her like a shadow, knowing whatever happened next might be the death of me.

Her hands found mine, drawing me closer. Together, we walked deeper into the unmarked forest, darkness blanketing us.

"Light, Eusebia," I whispered. We were far enough away from the others that her soft glow wouldn't be noticed.

"How come you never flare?" Eusebia asked. She was surrounded by a nimbus of light, just enough to enclose the two of us in it like a tight-fitting glove.

"You don't know?" My voice was gruffer than I'd meant it to be, but my ears were burning again, plainly visible to her in the soft light. I didn't want to talk about this, not with her.

"I know your light production is low," she answered. "But I've *never* seen you flare your light. It's unusual."

"Not just low," I answered, my hand tugging at my hair again. Gods Above, if my ears burned any hotter, it'd set my hair on fire. "Criminally low, Eusebia. I can't get through a single day on my own."

Eusebia frowned. "But Colias..."

"Colias shares with me twice a day. If he didn't, I'd likely die in the night."

There. I'd said it. Now she knew my shame. I waited for her to turn and walk away. Or maybe, she'd insist we walk together, knowing the shadow creatures could take me as easily as a downlander. But then there would be no more looks, no more hand-holding. She'd look at me like everyone else did. With disgust.

Instead, Eusebia leaned forward and rested her head against my chest. I was so shocked that I didn't raise my arms to encircle her, I just stared down at the top of her head like she was a wild animal.

"It shouldn't matter, but I know it does," she whispered. Her arms looped around my waist and she didn't seem to notice that I hadn't returned her embrace.

I raised my hands to set them gently on her back. I could feel the silky length of her single braid between my fingers.

Of course I wanted to kiss her. I wanted to hold her tight and explore every part of her body and mind. But I was already on borrowed time. She would eventually belong to someone else, and so I didn't allow myself more than this. A quiet embrace in the dark. Maybe it was my pride as a man, or maybe it was my fear, but I *couldn't* allow more than that.

After a few minutes, she let go, and I drew the first breath in what felt like an eternity. She laced her fingers through mine and we walked back to the campfire. Just before we reached the others, she stopped to look up at me. Her honey-colored eyes were bright and large.

I waited, expecting her to say something. Instead, she fed her light into me where our fingers touched. It was a gentle flow of light that swept away the darkness inside of me the way the first spring rush of water cleans away dead fall in a river. I blinked, unable to speak in the face of it. *Good* had been far too tame a word for the feel of Eusebia's light. It was like the first wildflower in spring, or a drink of water after a long day in the heat. It was a warm fire in the dead of winter, or a sweet summer rain. It changed me down to my toes, and I knew then that the moment her fingers left mine, I would likely die from it.

Eusebia gasped, a quick intake of breath that I would have missed if I hadn't already been staring down at her. My brow creased and I looked down at our joined hands.

And froze.

I was glowing.

Eusebia was looking me over as if she'd never really seen me before. Truthfully, so was I. I'd had so little light most of my life that I hadn't seen myself like this. But now I was glowing from head to toe like a candlewick.

Our eyes met again. I didn't know what to say, so I kept my mouth shut. Eusebia's eyes couldn't have gotten any bigger in that moment, my own light reflecting in the liquid pools.

Her light churned through my veins like a rushing river, and I took her other hand and fed light back to her. We were a closed system, her light pouring into me, and mine pouring back into her. As it came rushing down to me, it felt like Eusebia, bright and fast and laughing. I wondered what it was like on the return journey. Did it still feel like hers, or did it change through the filter of my body?

She pulled away, quickly. The light snuffed out like a blown candle, and I blinked, my eyes struggling to adjust to the change in light. Why had she pulled away?

She was scurrying back to her bedroll. I stood there like an idiot, gaping after her. Then my eyes skated over the others and I realized why she had pulled away.

Colias was awake. He'd seen everything.

Chapter Twelve

Colias seemed to make it his mission to keep us apart after that. The light he fed into me was heavy and suffocating, and I labored under the weight of it. Now I understood. The light people shared was tinged with their emotions. And Colias was angry. This was his punishment.

I didn't argue. I deserved it, and more. I'd told him that I'd do nothing and lightsharing with a girl who was not your fiance was an unforgivable breach of conduct. I hadn't understood it before. Didn't healers lightshare with strangers all the time? I'd been living off of borrowed light from benevolent healers, both male and female, for my entire life. It hadn't seemed any more emotional than if we'd been passing firewood between us.

Now I understood. Sharing light with Eusebia seemed to have changed me on some fundamental level that I'd spent every day since trying to unravel. I felt that I knew her in some intangible way, and I suspected she knew me in the same mysterious way. I avoided her gaze, and didn't allow a second of alone time between us. My chest had been ripped open unawares, and I was uncomfortable with what she might see there.

I spent as much time as I could alone, climbing trees to scout ahead or riding a plethron behind the rest of the group, guarding our rear.

Tor seemed to know that something had happened, but he said nothing. He sent me away from the group on the flimsiest of excuses.

I spent a lot of my time practicing my cuts. Colias was feeding me plenty of his punishing light, so I had enough to spare. Despite the lack of light, I'd always had good control. On this trip, I became lethal, drilling every spare moment until I fell exhausted in my bedroll at night.

Lasha was giving me long looks during the day, but she, too, said nothing.

It was a dark, early morning, and we were a day out from Lux when I was lagging behind the group, practicing my cuts again. Colias had filled me up to the brim an hour before and I had actually staggered under the weight of it. Now I bled it off in short bursts of light, trimming trees along the path.

Listen.

I grew still, drawing my horse to a stop. I strained my ears, listening for anything out of place.

Thwack!

I snapped my head to the west. Something was moving toward us. I let out a whistle for Tor, and guided the horse in the direction of the sound.

The sound of tree limbs snapping in quick succession had me picking up my pace.

Then a roar rattled the forest, and my blood turned to ice.

There was a scream behind me on the path. I jerked the horse around and kicked him hard into a gallop.

How did it get behind me?

My heart was in my throat. That roar could only mean one thing: a breacher.

"Cunigast!" Eusebia shouted.

I bent low in the saddle, goading the horse faster and faster. Eusebia's call lit my body on fire.

I broke through the treeline to a scene of madness.

A breacher was among the others. Colias and Tor were fighting madly, throwing off flashes of light the way an archer loosed arrows. Lasha was pinned under a fallen tree branch, and she was kicking furiously to win herself free. Naomi and Eusebia were standing together, arms linked. Naomi was pale, but Eusebia looked fierce, a knife ready in her hand.

Why had no one flared on the breacher?

My eyes met Eusebia's across the clearing. She turned and whispered in Naomi's ear. Both girls looked at me in a fierce way, though I had no idea what to make of it. I started moving toward them, throwing a few shallow cuts into the monster. It irritated the thing more than harmed it. Tor landed a significant blow that sawed off a limb, though a new one sprouted to take its place within a blink of an eye.

Eusebia reached for me, and so did Naomi. Without asking or waiting, they both began feeding light into me. I closed my eyes, the rush of light burning me like I'd been thrown into a fire. When I opened them again, I was aflame with the borrowed light.

"End this, Gast!" Eusebia whispered. I saw then that Naomi had been injured, her arm hanging at an unnatural angle from her shoulder. Dislocated, if I had to guess. Then the girls were pushing me forward into the fray.

I joined in with a will. The light thrumming through my veins made me quick as a hawk and light as air. I dashed forward, light flaring madly, and sliced at the breacher until there was nothing left to regenerate. In the cloud of ash that was left floating in the air, I looked up to see Tor and Colias staring back. They were both panting hard and red-faced.

"What were you two waiting for?" I snapped.

It was the wrong thing to say. I knew it as soon as the words were out of my mouth, but I could do nothing to drag them back.

"I was out! I'd just given all of my extra light to you, idiot!" Colias growled, his red cheeks reddening more. He spit at my feet, and strode away, making almost as much noise as the breacher had.

Tor stared at me a moment, sizing me up.

"See to the horses, boy."

The light the girls had lent me was already gone. I sagged under the strain. Taking in so much light at once was hard on a body, expelling it so quickly just as bad. I could sleep for days.

Instead, I squared my shoulders and turned back. I tended to the horses, though every brush stroke felt like an injustice.

Tor lifted the branch off of Lasha. She was mad as a hornet, but unharmed. Eusebia reset Naomi's shoulder with a pop that made me feel nauseated. No wonder the girl was pale as fresh milk.

The moment Colias crossed back into the clearing, I felt it like a knife in the back. If looks could kill, I'd be dead on the spot. He shared a word with Tor, who nodded once. Then Tor began making his way toward me.

"He doesn't want to lightshare with you right now. Do you need me to top you up, boy?"

I nodded. I'd stopped what I was doing, but I hadn't turned toward him.

"I was trying to let him take down the breacher. You stole the kill out from under him, lad. That's why he's so angry."

"I didn't know," I said.

"Course you didn't," Tor answered quickly. "Eusebia wasn't meant to call out for you like that. She went against orders, in fact."

"Will she get in trouble?" I asked, finally turning toward him. His hand slid off of my shoulder.

"She should," Tor answered with a shrug. "I'm leaving her to Lasha."

Chapter Thirteen

Lasha made Eusebia ride in the rear guard for the remainder of the trip, which felt like more of a punishment to me than her. Maybe that's why Lasha did it. She was canny like that.

Tor decided that one breacher was enough excitement, and so we turned back that same day. We made the return trip without incident. Colias continued to lightshare with me, but his resistance to the arrangement was tangible. The pounding punishment of light was over. Now I received a trickle, barely enough to keep me alive or him from a fatal light flare. Maybe this was his punishment to himself as well.

I assumed that as soon as we were back in camp, he'd request a partner change. I couldn't blame him, really. I'd stolen his moment of glory. It didn't matter that it had been an accident.

I fingered the bandana at my neck. When we got home, the elders would dye a stripe on it. I could hardly credit it. My first run, my first kill.

My first kiss.

Eusebia and I did not sneak away in the dark again. I lay awake at night forcing myself to stay in place.

No, that was a lie. I lay awake longing to run away with her. It was a fool's dream, and I knew it. There was no future for the two of us. No future with anyone for me. Heva's knife had doubled and trebled in weight.

We were one day away from home camp when I found myself a distance away from the others. We had all stretched out in a long line like beads on a string. Eusebia was the last bead on that string, and I realized that if I let my horse drag a little more, I could be alone with her for a moment or two. Colias, my watcher, had bunched up next to Naomi. Maybe he was hoping to steal a moment alone with a girl himself?

Eusebia's horse caught up to mine at a bend in the path. We were as alone as we'd ever been, except for that moment under the water.

I turned my horse sideways on the path. When she saw me, she drew hers alongside, flank to head, so that we were facing each other. I met her eyes in silence. I don't know what I wanted from her, what I expected.

What she offered was an embrace. She didn't ask, just leaned forward and pulled herself over onto my horse. Her arms were around my neck, her mouth on mine. The smell of her filled my senses, and for a moment there was nothing that was not Eusebia in my arms. My heart expanded as wide as the land in that moment, and contracted to the shape of her body.

"Run away with me," I whispered. We were short of breath and panting. Her cheeks were bright with color, and her eyes were as liquid-large as the night we'd lightshared.

I didn't realize what I'd said until I'd said it. Didn't realize I meant it until the words were out, hanging precariously between us.

"You have enough light for both of us," I went on, though I could feel my heart, newly-shaped, quivering with fear. "I can take care of you in all the other ways, Eusebia. And I will. I'd consider it an honor to care for you the rest of my days."

Eusebia's eyes widened, and filled with tears. She was shaking her head, even as they spilled down her cheeks. She held my face between her hands, her fingers in my hair.

"I'm so sorry, Gast. I'm so sorry that I can't leave with you. You have to believe me," she said, still crying. She kissed me again. "I wish so badly that I could. I'd choose you again and again, if it weren't for my family."

My fragile heart couldn't take her confession. I kissed her back once, gently disentangled her fingers from my hair, and set her back on her own horse.

"I love you, Eusebia. I probably always will," I said. Then I turned my horse and put heels to his sides.

Wait. Go back.

I can't. I can't!

Head down alongside the horse's head, I galloped. I wasn't sure where I was going, only away. I trusted my horse to stay on the path. I couldn't see it any longer, my eyes far too blurry with tears.

It was the first time I had ever disobeyed The Voice. It was not the last time.

Part Three

Chapter Fourteen

The elders dyed that stripe on my bandana. There was a bit of a fuss about it. Colias's family didn't attend the celebration, refusing to celebrate a kill they believed I stole from their higher light-producing son. They argued that I'd stolen light from the girls to kill that breacher, which meant it wasn't my kill at all.

I was surprised down to my core when the elders decided in my favor. It was my kill, no matter who provided the light. If Colias had been on site already, it was his own fault for not acting soon enough. I found out much later that Tor argued my side to the elders, and since he was a first-hand witness, it carried the day.

I was even more shocked to learn that Lasha had defended me just as fiercely outside of the elder's council. She made a request of the elders herself to bring me with her and Tor on future runs.

At the same event that celebrated my breacher kill, the elders announced Eusebia's engagement.

After the announcements, I went to the elders and requested to be put on the highest rotation of runs possible.

Tor and Lasha welcomed me on their runs. They extended to me a kind of respected kinship. Tor relied on me as a long scout, and Lasha trusted me with horses like no other. That suited me just fine.

After a series of runs with them, word spread to others that I was reliable. Other groups started requesting me. New runners wanted me for my experience. Old runners wanted me for my scouting abilities. I was steady and hard-working. I began adding stripes to my bandana, and that carried weight with old and new runners alike.

Eusebia married the man the elders gave to her. She started having children of her own. When I was in camp, which wasn't often, I occasionally saw her out with them. One by the hand and another on her hip. She still laughed with others, still extended her easy joy in a lazy circle that was as good as a lightshare, if it had come from any other person. I cringed away, because it was a painful reminder of what I had lost.

What I had never had, really.

Colias requested a new light partner even before I got my stripe. I wasn't surprised.

My next light partner was a man named Ashwin. He was quiet and secretive. He'd come to Iron Camp from another camp, so far away that I'd never even heard of it. Some place over the mountains called Snow Camp. He spoke with an odd lilt and didn't seem to mind that I took and took but never gave back light.

Ashwin turned out to be the perfect light partner for me. He was happy to go on however many runs I wanted. He was steady, if not spectacular on the runs. He spent most of his time hiding from everyone, usually climbing as high as he could into a tree and sitting there until we shouted up that it was time to move on. He was a keen hunter and could fell a deer or a rabbit at a hundred paces. I'd never seen anyone strike truer with their light.

Twice a day he would lightshare with me, and the light he fed into me was constant and pure. It was completely devoid of emotion. I felt good, vibrant with the generous load of light he poured into me. I could run for hours on foot or ride all day after a quick lightshare from Ashwin.

In camp, he disappeared. He would appear on my doorstep in the morning, share light, and then I wouldn't see him again until the next day. I wondered what he was doing with his time, but he was reluctant to tell me. I left him to his devices.

A quiet brotherhood formed between us. With a look or a nod, we could communicate an intention between us on the road. He didn't seem to require a lot of words, and I was comfortable with silence.

One morning, home after a particularly long run, I pushed open my cabin door to find Ashwin already waiting. He sat on the porch, his feet propped on the rail, hands resting on his flat stomach. Neither of us could seem to gain much weight, and I saw that his shirt sleeves were three fingers too short for his arms. Had it always been like that? I couldn't say.

"Morning, Ashwin," I said, handing him a mug of tea and settling myself down on the porch steps. The morning was misty and cool, a thick fog blocking our view of the deep forest ahead.

Ashwin sipped at the tea, otherwise motionless. I'd expected him to take two sips, share some light, and leave. It was what he usually did. Today, he lingered after sharing light. I raised an eyebrow at him. It was all the indicator he needed.

"Got assigned a fiance last night," he said. I nodded. So that's what was eating at him.

"Know her?" I asked.

He huffed in answer. I don't know why I asked. He barely knew anyone in camp. I'd had to remind him of Lasha's name for the first three runs we went on with her and Tor.

"Will you quit running?" I asked. It was a fair question. A lot of people did once they were married. But a knot of anxiety was already forming in my stomach over the idea. I couldn't imagine anyone else in camp tolerating me as a light partner half so well, and I couldn't bear to stay in camp all of the time. I *had* to go on the runs, to come up for air.

"Not sure. Probably not," he answered. He finished his tea, set the mug down, rose to his feet and gave me a nod. That was it. He was gone.

He'd informed me, in his usual recalcitrant way, what I needed to know. The rest would just have to wait.

I washed and dressed and light-footed it up to the camp square. Tor and Lasha were there, just stepping out of the elder councilhouse as I crossed the empty square of

105

communal space at the center of camp. I raised a hand, catching Tor's attention.

"Hey, boy!" he said, waving back. "Good to see you out in the sun."

"Ashwin told me this morning he's engaged," I said without preamble. Tor was nodding before I finished the statement.

"Minette, from here in camp. Do you know her?" he said. I nodded. She was a quiet girl with dark features and a petite figure. Her father was one of the head mine workers, a respected man. Her mother had produced a horde of children all of middling light production.

"Will he need to quit running, do you think?" I asked. Tor's eyebrows rose, as if he hadn't considered it.

"I suppose that will depend greatly on Minette," he said, rubbing at the wiry beard he insisted on wearing despite his wife's complaints. "Lasha is the only light partner I've ever wanted. She likes runs nearly as much as I do. We never missed a run, even right after we wed. Maybe Minette will be the same."

"But if she is, unless she has a light partner that will go with her, she'll become his light partner, won't she?"

Lasha and Tor shared a look. Lasha nodded once, and parted. Tor looked back at me with the same look he used to judge horseflesh. I braced for whatever he would say next.

"Here's the thing, Cunigast," Tor said. "Ashwin has enough light to share with you *and* a wife. Minette has a respectable amount of light. Occasionally she needs extra, occasionally she has extra to give. Mostly she is fine on her own though. Ashwin, on the other hand, always needs someone to bleed light off on. That's why you were paired in the first place. I doubt you need to worry about finding a new light partner just yet."

My eyes widened, but then I shuttered the look. My lips slammed shut, my mind trying to read between the lines.

The elders didn't want to foist me off on anyone else. Ashwin was getting a wife who wouldn't need much from him, just so that he could continue as my light partner. Did he know that? Did Minette?

Tor's hand landed heavily on my shoulder and squeezed.

"You're welcome to run with me and Lasha as much as you like, no matter who your light partner is, Cunigast."

It was a kindness, and it humbled me.

He walked away, and the absence was like air on a wound after the bandage was first pulled away.

You aren't alone.

I flinched. I didn't hear The Voice as often these days. Or maybe I just didn't want to.

I looked around the square. Lightwalkers were coming and going all around me. I'd been born in this camp, known most of these people the entirety of my life. No one stopped to speak with me. No one even glanced my way.

Yes, I am.

Chapter Fifteen

Ashwin continued running.

It was a relief to me that marrying Minette had changed nothing. Ashwin was the same in every way that I could see, only his address had changed.

Ashwin's light production was higher than any of us had realized, myself included. Minette took light from him as often as she could, a behavior I found odd until I remembered that moment with Eusebia, years ago. Regardless, Ashwin still shared with me once or twice a day in camp, and often three or four times a day on the trail.

We were camped on the side of the road. Tor and Lasha had brought a couple of first-time runners, a pair of girls who watched the trail as if they expected a daybreaker to come striding down it at any moment. I expected both girls to request this be their last run once we got them back home.

"I think she's favoring her front left hoof. What do you think?" Lasha asked, eyeing the horse professionally. She had asked me to look over her little horse, which she'd hung with the ridiculous moniker, Chickadee. I rubbed at the horse's shoulder, running my hand down the leg. Well-accustomed to my touch, she lifted the hoof, and I gave it a look. I took out my knife, scraped the inside clean and checked the frog and heel for defects. It looked healthy and intact. I let go and she shifted from foot to foot.

Tugging on her lead line, I walked her in a short circle.

There, I thought, spotting a ripple in her shoulder, and slight favoring in her leg. Lasha was right.

"I see it," I said. Lasha was nodding as well. "Do you have any of that liniment on you? The kind Shelly makes?"

"Of course," Lasha said. "Only carry Shelly's." She fished it out of her bag and tossed it to me. I scooped a glob out of the tight-lidded jar and began rubbing the horse's shoulder down. It smelled of cloves and grease. I'd have to find a stream to wash my hands or I'd smell that all day long. Patting Chickadee's grey flank, I handed the liniment back.

"Keep an eye on that. We'll need to go slow for a day or two. Give her a bit of a rest," I said.

"I'll tell Tor," Lasha said, turning to do just that. I caught Tor's attention from across the clearing and jerked my head to one side. *Heading out of camp.*

He nodded his understanding, then tapped a finger to his ear. *Keep an ear out for trouble.*

I nodded back.

It was nice to have a shorthand with people. I turned and headed into the woods, listening for movement that sounded out of place.

We were moving south, hugging close to the mountains, the way we had on that first run years ago. I followed a rise in the land, remembering a narrow stream somewhere close to here. A few yards into the forest, I paused and listened. The tell-tell trickle of water rewarded my ears. I started moving in that direction.

I walked for ten minutes, following the rise up and up. The land cut away sharply, and I looked down at a narrow, quick stream churning below. I started looking for a clear path down toward the water.

Look up.

I did it without thinking. The trees had cleared away until I could see the sweep of forest through which I'd just tracked. The rise had been sharp enough that now I could see the treetops over our temporary camp.

I sucked in a breath, surprised.

Ashwin was clearly visible, sitting at the very top of a tree. He was glowing bright as a coal, the light rolling off of him enough to compete with the sun.

Gods Above! He's already shared with me twice today!

I realized then that even the high estimates about his light production were too conservative. Ashwin was shedding light faster than most could absorb in a week.

How was that possible? I blinked hard, checking my vision, but it was undeniable. And if this was what Ashwin was doing even half of the time he spent alone in the treetops...

The realization staggered me.

What do I do with this knowledge?

Nothing. Just know it.

I suspected I'd obey The Voice this time as well, whether I agreed or not. No one would believe the truth.

Chapter Sixteen

Before we could return home, we encountered a breacher. Those two girls nearly took off running before Lasha could round them up like a herd of sheep. Ashwin was up in a tree when it happened, and he dropped down behind it like a squirrel, light already flaring. The rest of us were made rather ornamental after that. I sighed a breath of relief, peering into the ash cloud left. No matter how many times I encountered these things, I never lost the gut-tightening tension they brought.

"Everyone alright?" Tor called out in his resounding tenor voice. I nodded to him, looking around for the others. Lasha was already moving in my direction.

"She's hurt," Lasha said. I didn't understand at first. The light we shared amongst ourselves also healed our bodies. Lightwalkers generally need only to lightshare to heal.

Until they don't.

There is a threshold beyond which lightsharing can't do enough to heal a wound. Often, it's because there is something wrong that needs to be corrected before it can be healed. A splinter, as little as it might be, is a Lightwalker's bane. We can't heal until it's removed. This was true on a larger scale too. A bone needed to be reset, shrapnel removed, before a lightshare will fix anything. A rare occurrence, but there was a reason the healer's tent was always open.

Ashwin was at my side, anticipating another need for his light. Together we crossed the damaged clearing to find one of the girls lying there. Her face was white and sweating, and she looked at us with pain clear in her eyes. Her light partner was crying, holding her hand.

"Don't lightshare, Nika," Lasha was saying.

"But she's hurting!"

"I know, but she can't take it yet!" Lasha snapped back.

I looked her over, and saw the problem. Her leg was broken, the large bone in her thigh horribly out of alignment.

"What happened to her?" I exclaimed. Her light partner's tears increased, and her lip wobbled.

"She spooked her horse. He knocked her leg in the process."

"Have you ever set a bone on a person?" Lasha asked me. She knew I had with a horse. We'd done it together, and it had been an appalling experience. The horse had died anyway, in fact.

I felt like I'd gone as pale as the girl on the ground.

"Nothing like this, Lasha!" I answered.

"You're the best we have at the moment," Lasha said, grimly determined.

"I can do it," Ashwin said at my shoulder. I was as shocked as Lasha when he went to his knees beside the girl, braced her leg against his torso, and worked the bone back into place.

The girl passed out; it was a relief. I couldn't imagine the pain she must have been in. Her light partner, Nika, rushed away and was sick behind a tree. Frankly, I was little better. The sight of bones moving under the skin was horrible. And the sounds! Gods Above, I'd hear those sounds in my nightmares!

Lasha was steady as the sun, supporting the girl and Ashwin in turns. Once it was done, she had a straight limb and strips of bandaging to splint it. It was rough work, this roadside healing, but done quickly and efficiently. I prayed to the Gods Above that I'd never have to witness the likes of it again.

We unanimously agreed to turn back instead of trying to finish the run. The poor girl, whose name I learned was Laela, was in pain even after repeated lightsharing. Ashwin began supplementing her light alongside her light partner. Together, they kept the girl topped off, but it was still three days before the long bone could support her weight.

Two days away from home, I was looking over Lasha's horse again when Tor walked up behind me.

"Did you know he knew healer's work?" he asked. I shook my head.

"I suspect there's a lot we don't know about him, Tor," I answered. I was thinking of all that light I saw pouring off of him. Tor shook his head, ran a hand over his face, and looked away.

"Gods Above that was awful."

I nodded. We both turned, looking over the rest of our group. Ashwin was sitting casually, Laela next to him. She watched him with a look not unlike a hawk watching a field for a mouse, but said little.

"Think there'll be trouble there?" Tor asked. He raised an eyebrow at me, and I knew that shorthand as well.

"He's a married man. I doubt we have much to worry about. Once we get back in camp, the hero worship will wear off. It'll be fine," I said. Though I had already had the same wonder. Laela rarely looked away from Ashwin. We had all noticed.

As for Ashwin, he hadn't changed. The only variation was his new habit of lightsharing with Laela along with Nika. He looked as impassive as when he did it with me, but I couldn't help but wonder if more was transferring than light. Laela certainly seemed to hope so.

Chapter Seventeen

Laela asked us in her quiet voice to escort her to the healer's tent when we returned, and I suspected that she really only wanted to extend her time with Ashwin. Even I had to acknowledge that what he'd done for her was mighty heroic. At some point someone would have to speak to the girl about it though. This couldn't go on.

After we'd dropped her off, I walked with Ashwin back to his place. As his light partner, it was likely my job to speak to him about the girl. I just couldn't think what to say to him. Ashwin looked as impassive as ever, and didn't pause to say goodbye when we reached his cabin. I shrugged. I guess there was no need to say anything to him after all.

My own arrival was less quiet. I had my saddle and travelling gear, lugging it all up to my cabin, when I realized someone was waiting for me on the porch. In the shadow of the porch, I could only see that the figure was female.

Eusebia? My errant heart thudded painfully.

But no. Of course it wasn't her. I set my gear down with a clank on the bottom step.

"Heva."

"Gast," she answered in an equally hesitant tone. There was no reason for the distance between us except my own reluctance to be under Roderic's roof. His disdain for us was too evident, despite the five healthy children Heva had given him. It set my hackles up to watch him watch her. As if he'd had to come down off his high mountain to be with her.

"I haven't seen you these last three runs," she continued. Her eyes were trailing over me, checking for changes or injuries, I supposed. "You've gotten thinner. I can bring you food tomorrow."

"That's not necessary, Heva," I was so tired of being someone that everyone else needed to take care of.

"At least come have dinner with us. Spend some time with your nephews, Gast. They miss you."

That's unlikely, I thought. Last I'd checked, the boys had all inherited their father's disdain. The girls were kind like Heva, but they seemed to have developed a wariness about me that I couldn't account for.

"Does Roderic know you're inviting me?" I asked. It was an unfair barb, and I winced when it hit.

"It's my house, too, brother. I'm not unhappy there. I wish you could see that."

"I'll come, if you ask it of me," I answered. It was all I could say.

"I do. Come now, in fact."

"Now?" I asked, gesturing down at myself. "I'm filthy with the road, Heva."

"I don't care. Change, if you must. I'll wait here."

With a sigh, I nodded and stepped around her. It was a matter of minutes to change my road weary gear for clean trousers and a linen shirt. The thicker shoes were traded for softer moccasins, and I retied my bandana around my neck. It was always good to remind Roderic who had the most stripes between us.

Heva looked me over again at the door and nodded her approval.

Something on her mind, that was evident. She said nothing on our walk to her cabin, though. Well, I was accustomed to waiting on closed-mouth companions. She'd tell me when she got good and ready.

"Uncle Gast!" shouted the children. Two boys and three girls came crashing off of the porch. I was shocked to see how high up they stood next to me. How long had it been since I'd laid eyes on them? Gods Above, Helm and Osuin must be near old enough for their first runs!

My eyes met Heva's over their shoulders. Is that what this was about? No wonder Heva looked so grim about the mouth.

The boys jostled for my attention, another surprise to me, and I strove to reward them with it unstintingly. They asked about my most recent run.

"Did you kill any breachers?" Helm asked, eager for details.

"My partner did."

"Gods Above! I wish I'd been there!" Helm exclaimed. "How did he do it?"

I gave them the details I could. They were each intrigued by the idea of dropping directly out of a tree to ambush a breacher. I cautioned them that the tactic wasn't without flaws.

"If you accidentally fall on the breacher, you're hollowed or dead before you hit the ground," I said seriously. "Practice the basics. That's always the best approach."

"Eh. Basics," Osuin groused. "My brain is like to drip out of my ears from drilling basics already."

I grinned and ruffled his hair. I knew how punishing a master Heva could be.

"Listen to your Ma. She made me who I am."

That pulled them up short. It was interesting to be treated with this newfound hero worship. I wondered how Ashwin had borne it from that girl so easily.

I thought about him sitting in that tree top. He was probably used to it.

Dinner was two rabbits roasted whole, a brown gravy that I could have never made myself, and yeast rolls that made my eyes water they were so good. Heva's two older daughters ducked their heads when I complimented the food, and I realized they were the ones who'd made it all. How close were they to runs and weddings? Surely they still had a few more years.

Roderic had not made an appearance at dinner. So, gone playing courier for the elders then? I didn't ask. The kids behaved no differently, so I assumed they knew what kept him away this evening.

After a flurry of activity once dinner was concluded, we all spilled out into the yard. Long shadows were starting, but Heva lit torches. Between the lights and the ephemeral glow of her children, we could dispose ourselves rather peacefully in the small yard she called hers. I sat on the porch step, and she eased herself down beside me. I realized she must be nearer to forty than thirty now, my big sister. There were gray hairs liberally splashed through her black braids, and a few spidery lines around her eyes and mouth. Otherwise she looked much the same as she always had.

"Helm and Osuin?" I asked without preamble.

"Osuin first," she answered. "He's up for his first run in the fall. Will you take him with you?"

I paused. "I don't choose the roster, Heva."

"But Tor and Lasha will, if you ask them."

"Roderic isn't gunning for him to run with someone?" I asked. Most fathers did.

Heva just stared at me, her eyes level and steady, boring a hole into mine.

"*I'm* asking you, Cunigast."

I looked out, watching Osuin and Helm wrestle in the dirt, smiles on their young faces.

"I'll speak to Tor in the morning," I answered.

"Thank you," she said, as if it were already decided.

"I'll guard him with my life, sister. I swear it."

"I know you will, brother," she answered. I pretended to not notice the tears glimmering in her eyes.

Chapter Eighteen

Minette dyed the new stripe on Ashwin's bandana herself, and presented it to him at a celebration four nights after we returned. Her cheeks pinked up a little when he leaned forward to kiss her cheek, then straightened to tie it around his neck. The color in Ashwin's cheeks remained unchanged. I was standing up with him, being his light partner, so I had a front row view. I wasn't surprised.

Still, Ashwin was behaving oddly. I couldn't quite put my finger on what had tipped me off. He still appeared on my doorstep every morning, ready to lightshare. He still barely spoke, and disappeared for most of the day.

Twice, I'd seen him walking out of the woods, but there was nothing odd about that either. Ashwin was known to disappear into the forest all the time doing Gods Above only knew what.

I'd long since given up my forest wandering habits. Most of my time in camp was spent training my horse, Obadiah. Occasionally I helped the trainers with other horses. And sometimes I helped with training the youngsters. The next generation of Lightwalkers didn't hold my light production against me. Or they didn't know. They only cared about the stripes on my bandana.

But Ashwin didn't join me. What was he doing all day? I couldn't imagine he was practicing his cuts. He was already deadly accurate.

Probably bleeding off all of that light, I thought somewhat glumly.

One morning, I rose to find Ashwin in his normal position, waiting on the porch. I handed him a mug of tea. He took three dutiful swallows, then set it down. He held out his arm and I grasped it against my own, fingers to elbows. He shared until I was bursting, a healthy glow spreading between our arms.

I nodded at him, and he nodded back. Then he stepped off the porch and walked away. I leaned over the rail, watching him go. Instead of turning back toward camp, he ducked off the path, into the woods.

Follow him.

I intended to, whether The Voice had spoken or not. I set down my own mug of tea and slipped onto the path into the forest a stone's throw behind my light partner.

He was moving quickly, in a determined direction that led him up a high ridge to the west of camp. He headed toward the abandoned mines, that old path I knew well. Ashwin set a blood-beating pace, like he expected to be caught in a crime.

Ashwin doubled and tripled back on his trail, then climbed a tree and went on an overhead path for a while. He used tricks I'd taught him to leave no trail. Whatever he was doing, he wanted to ensure no one followed him. I doubted anyone other than me could have.

There was a quick-moving stream that tumbled down the mountain in a fall near where the marked path veered toward the old mine, a lesser cousin to the waterfall I visited. Ashwin paused at the fall, leaning back to peer up to where the water left the mountain side and jumped into freefall. Without warning, light burst from him like alcohol tossed on a campfire. I shielded my eyes, the brightness was so intense. He shed off enough light to burst, and for a panicked moment I wondered if that was what he'd intended. Had I followed him out here to watch him commit suicide? Gods Above, I hoped not!

But the light dialed down, in gradual, controlled stages. I felt my chest loosen. Ashwin was still alive, though he glowed like a firefly. I could look at him again. His black hair fell back to his shoulders, and the thin linen clothing he had donned were almost transparent with all of the light leaking through. A coil of envy settled in my stomach. How my life would have gone differently if only I'd had a fraction of the light he carelessly spent out here in the silent forest!

I considered leaving then. Surely there was nothing else for me to see. But then Ashwin shut down his light, and turned toward the path. He settled himself just below the entrance to the old mine, his back to a tree, arms crossed over his chest. I recognized this position. It was his guard duty position, though what he was guarding, I couldn't fathom. I knew him well enough to know that he could hold this position for hours.

It didn't take hours though. Not half a turning after Ashwin settled in his spot, footsteps came running up the path. I was shocked beyond belief when Laela appeared a moment later.

She wasn't surprised to see Ashwin there. Laela stepped off the path right where he was waiting as if they had planned the encounter. Ashwin rose to his feet, and she walked directly into the circle of his arms.

My silent, taciturn light partner held Laela to him like she belonged there and laughed. His entire face was transformed by the action. I wasn't close enough to hear what words they whispered to each other. The joy plain on his features though. Laela was smiling up at him, all of her hero worship replaced by something weightier.

They kissed once. Ashwin held her face between his hands and bent to kiss her a second time. Then came the light. It was shedding off of him, a calm and steady glow that could have fed four Lightwalkers for a week.

I had seen enough.

I had seen too much.

I turned and fled, wishing dearly to forget everything I'd just seen.

Why did you bring me here to see this?

The Voice was stubbornly silent though.

Chapter Nineteen

My mind was reeling about what I'd seen in the forest. Ashwin, silent and taciturn Ashwin, was having an affair. Gods Above! I could scarcely credit it and I'd seen it with my own eyes!

I spent a lot of time in the woods, cutting down branches. I only trudged back into camp when I was in danger of losing all of my light. For the first time in years, I found myself begging light from the healers again.

Ashwin, of course, was nowhere to be found.

The healer's tents were long, low and white. One long side was rolled up, open to all. I stepped up as long shadows were just beginning. I'd blown off some steam, but too much light. I couldn't last the night without help, and my pride wouldn't allow me to go knock on Ashwin's door just now.

Or maybe it was cowardice. What if Minette answered the door? How could I face her?

Laela was there. I had no idea she was training to be a healer, but there she was, standing at the tent's edge, white apron tied over her Lightwalker clothes. We looked at each other for a long moment. I ran my thumb along the inside of my knuckles, nervous. I could practically see the question on her face.

Does he know?

I looked her in the eyes, thinking my answer. *Yes.*

There was a flush of color in her cheeks, and she stammered over the typical greeting.

"Do you have a need for a healer?" she asked.

"Just some extra light," I answered, my voice low. I looked away. It was hard to be haughty when I was a beggar.

"But Ashwin..."

"I can't go to Ashwin at the moment," I answered quickly. My eyes darted toward hers, and away again. "He'll come see me in the morning. I just have to get through the night."

"Of course," she said, and held out her hands. I flinched. Could I accept light from her? Healers were trained to offer the most impersonal lightsharing experience possible. It had never bothered me before. But I kept flashing back to that moment, with Laela in Ashwin's arms.

Reluctantly, I placed my hands in hers. It was a quick exchange, just the barest of flashes. There was no emotion passed from her to me. I wondered if she picked up any of my reluctance.

"I'm sorry, Cunigast," she whispered. There was no more light passing between us, but she held my hands captive. "I love him more than life. I love him more than the breath in my own body. I can't give him up. I'm sorry if we've hurt you, though. He speaks highly of you. It would crush him if he knew that you knew."

I stared down at her, shocked. If the tent pole had jumped up and spoken so fiercely, I couldn't have been more surprised. This was like an entirely different woman, this person holding my hands between hers. Her eyes were bright, her cheeks flushed. She had spoken with steel in her voice. She sounded more like Lasha than the mild girl I'd met on the trail.

I disentangled my hands from hers, and walked away. I couldn't think of a single thing to say to her.

Chapter Twenty

Ashwin was the same in every way noticeable. I struggled to meet his eyes when he presented himself at my cabin every morning. Gods Above, it wasn't even hard to avoid his eyes. Without realizing it, we had established a relationship that didn't involve speaking, or even looking at each other. Who had started that? Him or me? I couldn't say now.

I should say something.

Laela's fierce insistence that Ashwin would be "crushed" if he knew that I knew resurfaced in my memory.

I shouldn't say anything. It isn't my business.

But the truth chafed at me all day long. I would have given anything for a chance to have a family of my own. Ashwin had been given one and it still wasn't enough. He'd gone and taken someone else's as well.

That was the reason for the taboos, after all. When a Lightwalker man and woman came together outside of their sanctioned marriages, it was understood that they were disrespecting the intended spouses of both. Unengaged Lightwalkers like myself were held to a slightly different standard, though no less exacting. I was expected to love no one, to be loved by no one. At least in a romantic way. I was allowed friendship, and it had blighted better be good enough because it was all I was going to get.

It was only a matter of time before Laela would be engaged to someone else in camp. What would they do then? Surely the madness would stop when she had a fiance? A husband?

"You're angry with me."

Ashwin's voice cut through my miasma. He was next to me on the porch step, his arm held out to lightshare. I was gathering wool again, and had missed the gesture entirely.

"I'm not," I answered, nearly choking on the words.

"You are. I can see it."

"I-" I stopped. How could I say it to him?

Ashwin met my eyes, and understanding dawned on him. I saw the widening of his eyes, the slump in his shoulders. His arm fell away.

"I see," he said. "So you know."

I didn't answer, just looked down at my feet. He was still next to me on the porch step. Our tea mugs were between us. I looked down at them. How odd that such a small space could feel like an ocean.

Instead of answering, I held out my arm again. Ashwin, looked away for only a second. Then he stretched his arm across that ocean to take mine.

The light that filled me up was not devoid of emotion, as I was accustomed to. Instead, it was full his feelings, a wild torrent of emotion that nearly swept me away. Anger and frustration, guilt and shame, but also, love and more love. Gods Above I could almost hear Laela's laughter in the light he shared with me. The brightness of that affection wove through all of the black that he was swimming in. It was a single gold thread in a storm of darkness. I was drowning in it, my own feelings growing numb under the immensity of feeling. I was-

He broke off the connection. I staggered, nearly falling over. What on the land could I possibly say to that swell of emotion? It was crushing!

"Are you walking around with that all the time?" I asked, gasping for air. I bent over and put my head to my knees. I swallowed down breath after breath but couldn't seem to catch enough air. My lungs couldn't labor under that pressure.

"Every second of every day," Ashwin answered miserably.

I raised my head to stare at him. I would have gone mad with it. I could feel it down in my bones. I would have gone mad *ages ago*.

I met his eyes and realized the truth. He *was* mad with it.

"Ash-"

"Don't, Cunigast," he cut me off. He was already rising to his feet. "I can't take your sympathy. I just needed you to understand. That's all."

I watched him walk away. I was more confused than ever about what to do.

Chapter Twenty-One

The rest of that week went in a blur. I asked Tor about Osuin, but didn't mention that he was my sister's son. Either Tor knew or he didn't. It was unlikely to matter one way or the other. When I got my orders for the next run, Tor met my eyes and gave me a nod. That was the only indication he made.

Osuin was on our next run, riding atop a fresh chesnut horse and looking as young as any runner I'd ever seen. It was earlier than Heva had expected, but she seemed willing to give up a couple of months of safety at home for a first run with me. The very idea staggered me.

Osuin seemed just as enamored with me and my runner reputation as he had at the dinner some time ago. He followed me around like the stripes on my bandana might rub off from proximity alone.

Osuin had a light partner the same age as himself named Gareth. They were both good boys, eager to go on their first run. They were certain of glory and swagger if they only could get out of the limits of Iron Camp. I understood them, having been much the same, if a shade more bitter, on my own first run. Their hubris was catching, and all of us were walking around with our chests puffed out before long. Even Lasha, the only woman on this run, was determined to educate them on her prowess. She never could turn down a challenge, and these boys were full of them.

Ashwin and I had not spoken more on the matter of his affair. His lightsharing had returned to the neutral, emotionless exchange it had always been. I wondered if it would have helped him if I'd agreed to take the emotion as well as the light. Would it blunt the edge of his madness?

I watched his exchanges with a newfound understanding. He wasn't rude or unfeeling. He was numb to the world. He was walking around so overwhelmed with his own feelings, he couldn't possibly absorb anyone else's as well. If that wasn't a kind of madness, then I didn't know what was. It was a wonder he could function at all.

Ashwin spent a lot of his free time in the treetops, as was his wont. Osuin asked me about that, but I deflected the question. He was easy to guide in conversation, happy to talk about whatever you wanted and curious about everything. Still, I found myself looking toward the upper canopy and wondering about my light partner like I never had before.

"Uncle Gast!" Osuin called. I wheeled my horse around to see him galloping up the path toward me. There was a smile on his face, so I knew it was good news he was carrying.

"Gareth found a baby raccoon!" Osuin said. His cheeks were flushed a healthy red, and I could see something of Heva in him. I reached out and ruffled his hair.

"Oh yeah? And what does he propose to do about it? Lasha can cook up a lot of things, but I think she might draw the line at baby raccoons," I answered. Osuin recoiled in horror.

"We want to *keep* it, not *eat* it!"

"My apologies," I answered with a laugh, knowing full well what they had intended from the start.

"Come on! Come look at it!"

He was already turning his horse around, no doubt in his mind that I'd come with him. I whistled once for Tor in the lead, and followed my nephew around the bend.

Gareth was on the ground at the edge of the trail, his arms gathered up against his chest.

"Can we keep it?" Gareth was asking before he could even show me the little creature. I looked down from my horse at the fuzzy bundle in the boy's arms. Seventeen. They were seventeen. I kept having to remind myself.

"Hand it here, then." I held out a hand. Gareth carefully deposited the creature into my outstretched hand. It was small and grey and filled my palm. Its eyes were open, and its tiny head swiveled toward me with interest. I held it steady against my chest.

"I don't know that Lasha will allow it," I said. "It's up to her though."

"Aw, Uncle Gast," Osuin started with a whine. "If you'd say it's alright, she'd allow it and you know it!"

"I do *not* know that," I answered. "Besides, it's a matter of respect. She and Tor are the senior runners on this trip, and tradition says we ask the most senior lady about pets."

"Who are you calling 'senior'!" Lasha called, coming around the bend with Tor. She was laughing before I could answer her.

"Well, let's see what you've found," Lasha said, pulling Chickadee up next to my Obadiah. She held out her hands, and I transferred the little warm body into them. As tough as she could be about so many things, Lasha had a soft spot for animals. I wondered if the boys knew they'd found *her* a new pet.

"Tell me, boys," Tor said in his carrying voice. "What were you doing off your horses that you found the little critter in the first place?"

"I had to..." Gareth started, his eyes cutting over to Osuin.

"Out with it, boy," I said, reinforcing Tor's command. Both sets of eyes snapped forward to me.

"Aw just tell 'em, Gar" Osuin said, making a face.

"Not in front of a lady!" Gareth hissed back.

Well, this should be good.

"I assure you there is nothing you boys can say that I haven't heard before," Lasha said, looking up from her new prize. "Spit it out."

Gareth was turning a peculiar shade of red, but he managed to put words together.

"I keep having to stop to... uh... answer the call of nature, ma'am."

"He's got the runs," Osuin smirked. "He's been sneaking off trail to do his business nearly every half turning."

"Every half turning?" I asked. "I hope you're drinking water. You'll get dehydrated pretty fast like that."

"I'm trying," Gareth answered miserably. "Seems like every time I take a sip of water, I have to go running off into the woods again though, er, sir."

I looked over at Lasha.

"Sounds like an illness, don't you think?"

"Anyone else feeling the same effects?" she asked around the group.

It was then I realized that Ashwin hadn't rejoined the group. I jerked my head to the side and Tor nodded. He'd already noticed. The old runner didn't miss anything.

I turned my horse and went down the trail. Ashwin was supposed to be guarding the rear. He should have caught up to us already.

My horse ate the distance easily and quickly. I turned toward the trees, looking for signs of him. Maybe he had the same ailment as poor Gareth, and was off attending to his own personal business. Still, Ashwin was a more experienced runner. He'd have mentioned it if he was going to be disappearing off the trail often.

I tilted my head back, taking in the treetops in my scan of the surroundings. Would he have gone up without telling us? Surely not.

I thought of the look in his eyes when he'd looked at me on my porch that morning.

Maybe the emotions had become too much, and he's disappeared to shed off some feeling as well as some light. It wasn't good protocol, but I could hardly blame him after experiencing that brief wash of crushing feeling.

A darker tremor ran through me. What if he had decided he couldn't bear the weight of it anymore? What if he had drawn backward on the trail to burst? The only sign that would be left would be his horse, and his talisman draped over the saddle horn.

"Ashwin!" I called, cupping my hands around my mouth.

"Here!" a voice called back. I drew my first breath in a minute. My heart restarted its beating. When had I become so terrified to lose Ashwin?

He appeared on the trail, guiding his horse along like usual. His expression creased in confusion when he saw me there, gasping in the middle of the trail.

"What's wrong?" Ashwin asked, drawing his horse up alongside mine.

"Nothing," I answered. It was the truth, but I knew it wasn't the answer he wanted. I saw it this time. His guard slid into place almost as soon as I said it. "Gareth found a baby raccoon. He's trying to convince Lasha to keep it. I thought you would have caught up to us already, so I came looking."

Understanding dawned on him, taking in the message between the lines as well. He held a hand out and settled it on my shoulder.

"Sometimes I lag far behind so I can bleed off some light," he answered the question I didn't ask. He did that often. I was only now noticing because I hadn't been looking for it before.

"Gareth is sick. I was worried the same sickness had overtaken you farther back on the trail." It was not untrue, but it wasn't what had shaken me up, and we both knew it.

"I'm not going anywhere, Cunigast," Ashwin answered, giving my shoulder a squeeze.

We turned our horses and went riding back to join the others at a slow pace.

"How do you cope with it?" I asked, hesitant. He knew what I meant.

Ashwin was silent. I assumed he just wouldn't answer. It wouldn't be the first time he outright ignored a question.

"Sharing helps a little," he said softly. "It's always been like this for me. I didn't know for a long time that others were different, you see."

"If it helps, I can…" I let my voice trail off. I could what? Take more light from him? He'd let his emotions color his lightsharing one time, and it had crushed me in seconds.

"She's the only person I've ever met that helps."

It was clear he didn't mean his wife. Gods Above, what a nightmare.

We were drawing close to the others. There was no chance for more discussion, and I was relieved. I didn't know what to say to him anyway.

Chapter Twenty-Two

I had been correct in my assumption. The boys were deflated when Lasha declared the raccoon hers, but mollified when she allowed them to carry it in turns. At night, the little creature could be found snuggled down with any of us. I'd even slept with it a couple of nights when the beast was so inclined. I had to admit that there was something pleasing about that warm weight sleeping on my chest.

Osuin showed himself to have decent light control. I anticipated that if he didn't sour with age, he'd be a good, solid runner in time. His light partner, Gareth, was a silly boy. He was shy and immature, but I could detect no unkindness in him. I expected that with time he'd become one of those steady types that never left the camps. Both had enough light that they would undoubtedly be assigned a fiance and end up with families of their own. These two would make it. They were going to have a straight and easy path in life, if only they would take it. I was proud of my nephew, proud for Heva, even if it was a little bittersweet for me.

Lasha looked over the boys with almost the same attention she took with the baby raccoon. Somehow they had won her over, something I'd never entirely done myself. If there were any doubts, those doubts were shut down when Lasha elected to trade at a downlander town for sweets to give the boys after dinner.

"You can't be serious, Lasha!" I exclaimed when she returned with them.

"What?" Lasha asked, indignant, arms laden with sweet rolls.

"We're meant to train them on the hard life of the trail, not fatten them up!" I was grinning though. Something about these two won hearts and made us want to dote on them. It was good to see that I wasn't the only one.

"I'll have you know this was Tor's idea!" she scoffed. I laughed out loud.

"You're both going soft," I said, still laughing. She started turning red, on the verge of throwing all of the sweet rolls to the ground.

"Soft!" she shouted indignantly. "I'm not going anything!"

I held my hands up in surrender. "I give! You're right. I'm sure you could still beat me in a foot race, too."

"Bet your skinny hindquarters on it," she answered, drawing herself up to the fullness of her small height. I laughed again.

The truth be told, I was hoping for a sweet roll for myself. I'd let her win at any contest she wanted.

That night we were disposed around the campfire, eating our sweet rolls when there was a crashing sound in the darkness.

I looked to Tor and Lasha. Ashwin was at my side, already poised for motion. The boys had been laughing, their faces sticky from the rolls, but now they were silent.

"Bear?" I asked Tor. There were plenty out in these woods, but they didn't often go roaming about this late into the evening.

"Maybe," he said, the single word stretched out long. The look he gave me said he didn't think it was a bear at all.

Of course runs were a coming of age tradition for all Lightwalkers. They were to teach everyone about the hardships of the trails, to know what runners were putting up with, but mostly it was to teach them about breachers. There was such a concentration of light near the camps that we didn't often get breachers near our borders. But in the downlands? They roamed the isolated areas like a plague, and it was our sworn duty to go out and kill them.

In theory, every run would result in a breacher's death. In reality, there were many runs where no one ever encountered a breacher. I'd met runners who had gray in their beard before they saw one for themselves. It was a reality that still shocked me. I already had four stripes on my bandana, and I'd watched Tor and Ashwin both take down more.

Every mother prayed to the Gods Above that her children never encountered a breacher on their customary run, then settled into a career in camp and was never in danger again. The look in Tor's eyes confirmed what I knew. Heva's prayers would go unanswered.

"Go look into it, Cunigast," Tor said. "I'll circle around to the north."

I looked to Ashwin and Lasha. "Stay with the youngsters?"

Lasha nodded, but Ashwin met my eyes. "I'll keep them safe. I swear it."

Ashwin was as clear-eyed as I'd ever seen him. Whatever concerns I might have about his madness, I knew he wouldn't fail me here. I reached out for his arm, and though he'd only given me light an hour before, I felt a surge of more fill my veins.

"Osuin, Gareth, don't move from this spot unless Ashwin tells you to," I said, leaving no room for argument. It was Tor's right to give those orders. I didn't care; this was my sister's child.

There was a snap in Osuin's gaze that told me everything I needed to know.
He knew it wasn't a bear. He wanted to follow me.

My gaze slid down to his cheeks, still sticky from the sweet rolls. *Not tonight, little nephew.*

I turned, trusting Tor to take his position in the darkness. I picked up my bow, though no one believed I'd encounter a bear.

Just out of sight, I dropped the bow. I started running.

There was another crash, then the bone-rattling roar that only a breacher could make.

In theory, fighting breachers was a group effort. In reality, it was often just one Lightwalker, ideally experienced and skilled, that faced the breacher. Others might give support, but generally the bulk of the work was to keep the group together, Lightwalkers as well as horses.

It was dangerous work, and injuries were common. Breachers often uprooted and threw whole trees. Staying out of a breacher's way was half the job. Fighting at dusk or dawn was common, more ideal. We were facing one in full dark, and that was the most dangerous of all. Breachers were capable of fading in and out of the darkness the same as their more ethereal counterparts, the shadow creatures. The darkness made them that much harder to track.

I'd seen new runners grip a knife when they went to face a breacher. Pointless, really. A breacher was solid enough to touch us, but not solid enough to feel a knife. As I walked into the dark forest, I flexed my hands. It was best to be loose and ready. There was a tightness in my chest that I had never been able to train away, but my limbs felt light and mobile.

Tor would circle to the north, and come behind the creature if he was able. That was a good tactic, and one we'd used more than once. One Lightwalker approached from behind, landing a direct cut that would, hopefully, distract the breacher. Then the point Lightwalker could come in with a strong flare and end it.

I braced myself to do just that, and tried to quiet all of my movements.

It didn't take long to find the creature. The thing was making a lot of noise. Its fluid body had four arms, each gripping a different tree and shaking for all it was worth. A scattering of loose branches fell like a thunderstorm was rolling through the boughs. I ducked to the side, narrowly missing a large branch that swung from above.

The breacher was heavy around the base, leaving a shadowy trail along the ground like an early morning mist. The thing howled, and I gritted my teeth. I was close enough now that the sound hurt.

Where are you Tor?

The breacher turned abruptly, upending one of the trees. A second tree followed, and the breacher tossed it forward like a father might toss a ball to a child. The second tree crashed loudly against another stand of trees.

Had Tor made the cut? It was now or never. I took in a deep breath, preparing to run forward and flare light.

Wait!

I was already in motion, and I stopped so hard that I fell backward, stumbling to a stop. My hands were roughed up by nearby trees that I'd hit, trying to catch my balance.

What now? I demanded of The Voice. *Tor is waiting!*

Tor is dead.

What?

I blinked hard. I couldn't process the information. If Tor was dead...

A second breacher came crashing through the trees, this one spindly and tall, three arms rotating around its middle the way the points rotated around a windvane.

There was a rushing sound in my ears. What on the land was I supposed to do about *two* breachers?

What do I do? What do I do?

Panic was setting in, and I shook myself. Lightwalker training had its place and mine was asserting itself. The tactics were similar no matter the number of breachers. We all knew it was possible, in theory. I'd never met anyone who'd seen two breachers. Did they fight together? Did they fight each other?

Peering through the darkness, I watched the two breachers undulating in the forest. They seemed to be ignoring each other. The second breacher disappeared into the darkness, and the hair on my arms raised. It was still there, just invisible.

I slipped sideways through the forest, circling around. How could I separate them? How could I flare twice?

I couldn't. I needed Ashwin.

Fine, then. Flare once. Find Ashwin and reload. Pray it's enough. Pray the others can get away. Gods Above, let Osuin get away from this!

I waited for the remaining visible breacher to move closer. I shouted, leaping forward, and the thing spun toward me. Another tree was gripped in one of its four arms, and it launched it at me.

I rolled away, dodging the tree. Trees were awkward weapons, their branches tangling with the ones still standing. This one was caught in a bough and the trunk end swung around toward me.

I sped forward, ducking under the dangling trunk end, and flared. Focused, my light shot out of me in a bolt that cut the monster in half. Four limbs and a tapering top end separated from its dense, shadowy bottom. Because the cut was clean through, the separated ends burst into an ash cloud.

A face full of ash greeted me, and I wheeled sideways to avoid the path of the second breacher.

It didn't matter. Visible again, the second breacher was close enough to see what had happened. It was already turning for me.

I wrapped an arm around a branch to swing myself around and run in the opposite direction.

What now?

Run north.

North? That's the direction I just came from!

Do you want to drive this thing toward Osuin?

North, it is.

I turned, circling wide around where the breacher was. It did not slow, but it wasn't particularly fast either. It turned awkwardly, its three arms gripping trees and using them to steer its shadowy base in a new direction. I wondered again why it was so hard to outrun a breacher. They were blighted awkward beasts!

We crossed into a clearing, and the breacher howled. I looked over my shoulder to see the creature galloping toward me faster than a horse. Its figure blurred, rolling forward like a wave.

Oh yes. That's why.

I ran for all I was worth. It was to no avail. The breacher was gaining, and fast.

What now? I went north! I shot the frustrated thought toward The Voice, but I knew the truth. I was going to die here. I was out of light. The fatigue of my first cut was already slowing my limbs. As soon as the breacher caught up to me, I'd be dead in moments.

I looked forward and realized light was waiting for me.

Ashwin was standing on the other side of the clearing, arms wide. The light was already gathering in his core.

Our eyes met. He jerked his head to the side, and I nodded once.

Speeding past him, I kept running. I didn't slow until I heard the roar.

Behind me, Ashwin flared, spearing the second breacher.

I was already moving toward the others. Toward Osuin. Surely the Gods Above wouldn't have kept me safe only to let him get hurt?

I burst into the circle of firelight to find Lasha guarding the boys, knife in hand, as if she expected a bear to come charging out of the night.

I stood gasping, my breath churning through my body in painful tugs.

"Are they okay? Are you okay?" I asked between gasps.

"We're fine. Ashwin took off like a bug was in his shorts and didn't say a blighted word. Cunigast, are *you* okay?" Lasha said, her eyes looking me over for injuries.

Our eyes met, and I realized what I had to tell her next.

"Tor."

Lasha went very still. She knew. We always knew before someone told us, didn't we? Lasha was already shutting down, the light going out of her eyes before I could say more.

"And Ashwin?" she asked, choking on his name.

"He's somewhere behind me." I stepped closer. I kept expecting her to fall, faint, or cry out. But this was Lasha.

"Lasha, there were *two breachers!*"

162

There was a flare of life in her eyes at that. She was looking over my shoulder.

"Is he?" She didn't have to say more. Is he hollowed? Is he gone? Is there a body?

"I don't know."

"I'm going to look."

She moved toward the darkness, leaving me staring at two boys over the campfire.

"What happened Uncle Cunigast?" Osuin asked. It was a far cry from the way he'd asked me about breacher kills before. This time he was afraid.

He should be afraid. I was afraid.

Ashwin appeared then.

"Lasha?" he asked.

"Looking for... Tor."

Ashwin nodded. He turned to follow her.

"Ash..." I stopped him. "How did you know?"

Ashwin looked at me, and I could see that glimmer of madness hovering over him.

"How did you know to turn north?" he asked.

Chapter Twenty-Three

Lasha turned our party around the next morning and we went home. She spoke little, cradling the raccoon against her shoulder almost like an afterthought. The boys were somber, and we kept our little group close together for the rest of the journey home.

The boys didn't want to be alone, and I didn't want to leave Lasha alone. She and Tor had loved each other, truly. How would she cope with his loss? I didn't think she was the type to go off and lightburst on her own, but you never really knew. I watched her closely, and counted the seconds she was out of sight.

Ashwin continued riding in the rear position, and I wondered if he was affected by the loss as much as the rest of us were. Probably.

I was starting to notice a lot about my light partner. He was observant. He was often in pain. He shared none of it. How had he managed that? I was certain I'd have lightburst a long time ago just from the strain. But he rose each morning and did his duty, silently.

Lasha had found Tor's talisman, and his favorite knife. I knew there was probably a pile of clothing buried in those woods, but I didn't ask her about it. These two things were all she had left of him, and she carried both on her person.

Every night, I thanked the Gods Above that I wasn't carrying a talisman back to Heva instead. The weight of the Heva's knife was a slight thing compared to the shame I shouldered alongside it.

Back in camp, a ceremony was held for Tor. Ashwin and I stood shoulder to shoulder and watched them add his name to the stone wall at the north end of camp. All Lightwalkers who died fighting a breacher were listed here. It was a proud tradition, and the entire camp turned out for the ceremony. No one knew who had built the wall, each stone was easily larger than a horse, and perfectly fitted together without mortar. There was one in every Lightwalker camp, though, and Lightwalkers had been etching their fallen's names on them for as long as anyone could remember.

A large oil brazier was lit in the center of town, and it was to be left to burn out on its own, in honor of Tor. The

gathering of people was a stark contrast to the lonely brazier
I'd lit for my father. Heva and I had stood together alone
before his. Lasha lit Tor's in front of the entire camp, men
and women standing with hands folded in front of them.

Lasha stood by the brazier all through the first night.

Osuin and Gareth brought their siblings out to touch
Tor's name on the wall, then to watch the light burning
down. It made me proud of the boys, even as it made my
heart tighten in my chest.

The second night, I stood in Lasha's place, just to get
her to sleep for a few hours.

The third, Ashwin stood.

The fourth night, we all watched the light flicker out,
and it was like he'd died all over again.

When I turned away from the dying light, I saw
Eusebia standing under the eave of a nearby building,
holding her own vigil for Tor.

The sight of her still stopped my heart. I shuttered the
feeling and walked slowly home in the dark. I didn't care that
I didn't have much light. I wouldn't have fought it if a
shadow creature had come to hollow me right then and there.

"You have to eat, Cunigast," Heva said. She was standing on my porch in the midday sun, staring down at me. I was sitting on a stump that I kept there for that purpose, leaning my back against the wall.

"I do eat, Heva," I answered her. But I knew what she meant. My shirts were dangling off of my shoulders again.

"You're a skeleton. Come with me. Now," she said. There was no room for argument.

I rose slowly, and followed, dragging my feet. I was being a brat. It didn't matter. She had the patience of a woman with five children, and it showed.

When we got to her yard, Osuin bolted out the front door and slammed into me with a hard hug. The boy's fierce affection was almost enough to render me to tears, and I sucked in a hard breath to hold back the feelings.

"That's enough, Osuin. We're okay, boy."

"I'm so sorry, Uncle Cunigast," he said, still holding on. "I'm so sorry about Tor. He was a good man."

Gods Above! Had I ever been this free with my feelings in all my life? The difference between us couldn't be measured solely in years.

"That he was, Osuin. That he was." I gripped his arms, and pulled him back to look him over. "But Tor of all people wouldn't want us making such a fuss about him. He'd tell you to train harder for next time instead."

"Is that what you're doing?" Osuin asked, looking directly in my eyes. "Are you training?"

The question gutted me. No. I'd been pouting like a child.

"I'm going to start today. After lunch. Do you want to come with me?" I asked.

Osuin nodded, wiped his tears and headed back toward the house.

I raised my eyes to see Heva looking me over again.

"That'll do, then," she said, and followed her son indoors.

I realized this was what she'd intended all along.

Chapter Twenty-Four

I trained Osuin every bit as hard as Heva had trained me. My sister must have been easier on her own children, because he was quite shocked when I bound one of his arms and insisted he fight me.

"Why are we doing this?" he exclaimed.

"What if you have to fight with one arm? What if you're hollowed before the breacher is killed?"

"Gods Above! Does that happen?" Osuin's eyebrows were up around his hairline.

"It can. And we have to be ready for anything. Now, fight me. Then we'll switch arms."

Training Osuin brought me more satisfaction than I would have imagined. It wasn't long before Osuin brought Helm as well, and I spent many happy hours with the boys, training in the yard in front of my cabin. The place had never been so full of laughter and joy.

Ashwin, on the other hand, was avoiding me.

He still came to lightshare, and I knew there was no danger of that ending. However, he didn't bother to sit when he came, and he left without sharing a word on most days.

"Ashwin," I said, after a week of his silence. "Are you really going to never speak to me again?"

"I thought you weren't speaking to me," he answered, his dark eyes raising to meet mine.

"I can't condone it," I said. "But I can't condemn you either. I don't know what to say about any of it."

"I doubt there's anything you can say," Ashwin answered. "I don't condone it either, if it makes you feel better. I just can't seem to stop."

I thought again about asking him to share his emotions as well as his light, but he was already walking away.

He was still seeing Laela. I'd seen her in the village square not two days ago, and she blushed furiously when she saw me. It was embarrassing, and I prayed to the Gods Above no one got the wrong idea about us. What a nightmare that would be!

I wanted to avoid the dilemma altogether, but the next morning it was waiting for me on my porch in the form of a person.

"Minette!" I exclaimed. She looked small and dark, her brow creased in worry.

"Cunigast, can I talk to you?"

"I guess so," I answered, panic already setting in. But like a fool, I stepped backward, allowing space for her to come inside. She scurried in as if expecting me to slam the door on her.

"What can I do for you?" I asked, praying this conversation would be short.

"Do you know where Ashwin goes every day?" she asked.

No beating around the bush then.

"Out to the forest, I think."

"What could he be doing out there, day after day?" she asked, clearly frustrated.

Was I a coward for not telling her the thing she would most want to know? Yes.

"Shedding light, mostly."

"What?" she exclaimed.

Oh. She didn't know.

"You know Ashwin produces an enormous amount of light, don't you?" I asked, desperate to sound casual. It almost certainly meant I sounded strained.

"I knew he produced more than most, but he shares with me every morning. I thought he shared with you twice a day?"

"Yes. More when we're on the trail."

"And he still has enough to bleed off all day in the woods?" she asked, her voice ratcheting upward.

"And then some, Minette." I ran a hand through my unkempt hair. It was early in the day, and I expected Ashwin to turn up at any moment. What would he say if he saw Minette standing here chatting with me? Likely nothing.

"That's...unheard of."

"I think it's something of a secret. I didn't know myself for a long time."

Minette's mouth snapped shut at that. A grimness fell over her expression, and I couldn't fathom what that might mean.

"Thank you for speaking with me, Cunigast," she said, and went for the door. It swung wide to reveal Ashwin standing on the porch.

Oh no!

I hung back, coward again, and waited for Minette to explain. She was the one who'd shown up unannounced. She was his wife.

"Minette?" Ashwin looked confused, then looked up at me.

"Don't look at Cunigast like that!" Minette snapped. "You won't tell me a blighted thing, so I came to your light partner to try to find out something. You disappear early in the morning, show up late at night. You never say a word to me, and you expect me to be okay with that?"

"I share light with you every day," he said, and he looked genuinely confused.

"We're married!" Minette shouted, the sound deafening in my silent house. "You should be sharing a lot more than a pittance of light in the dark early hours with me!"

Ashwin had gone very still and pale, his hands frozen at his sides. Minette was vibrating with her anger, and I sincerely longed to be anywhere else. I'd fight a breacher to avoid being in this room at this moment.

"I-" Ashwin started, then stopped. There was nothing he could say, was there? Everything she was saying was true. And he likely wasn't sorry.

Minette made a helpless noise, choking back on angry tears, and shoved him aside. She stormed away, leaving Ashwin and me looking at each other like fish out of water.

"You should probably go after her," I said.

"And say what?" Ashwin asked.

"I haven't a clue," I answered honestly. "But it's not her fault you didn't want her. She didn't choose you either, you know."

Ashwin blanched. He stepped closer, and for a moment, I thought he would hit me.

Instead, he gripped my arm and fed light into me. This light was a bit more tainted with his emotions than usual, but not the fully open floodgate of feeling I'd experienced before. I felt his confusion, his frustration. I felt the helplessness he was experiencing, and I could sympathize. I felt pretty helpless myself.

"Sorry," he said, nodding toward where our arms met. Then he turned and walked away.

"What are you going to do?" I asked, following him onto the porch.

He paused, then looked back at me. "Do you really want to know?"

"Yes," I answered, certain I'd regret it.

"I'm going to ask Laela what to do."

Chapter Twenty-Five

As I'd predicted, Osuin wanted to continue with runs and his friend Gareth did not. Fortunately for Osuin, his brother Helm was as mad as he was to go on runs. Helm was given special permission to go on his first run earlier than usual, and Osuin had agreed to partner with him. The brothers had been sharing light for some time, and it seemed a logical and natural pairing.

I had been training the boys as often as I could, so it was also a logical decision for the boys to go on their first run with me. The elder council suggested it before I could make the request.

Lasha had opted to retire from runs for a while. I wondered how she would adjust to the pace of camp life after so many heady runs. I visited her several times following Tor's death, checking in on the woman who'd been an advocate for me for so long. She could return a smile, but it was wan. She still had the raccoon, and she'd named it Nanook, some name Ashwin had taught her from his people in faraway Snow Camp.

"I'm fine, Cunigast. Quit trying to mother me. You're terrible at it," she'd told me. I took it as a good sign. If she could get annoyed, it was only a matter of time before she was back to herself.

Despite all that had happened and the number of stripes on my bandana, I was still surprised when the elder council asked me to begin leading runs. I'd expected to follow another leader forever, but the truth was I had more experience than any other two runners put together. I had the most stripes in our camp. I was recently turned twenty-seven, it was more than time for me to be a leader. I shouldered this new responsibility with some trepidation.

"Are you really surprised?" Ashwin asked me later.

"I am."

"I don't know why," he said. "You're the best runner in camp."

"Not better than Tor and Lasha."

"You're the only one who thinks that. Even Tor thought you were better. Told me so himself."

That shut me up quick. Ashwin didn't joke much at the best of times. He was deadly serious now.

Most of the village still avoided me as if I were carrying some downlander disease. The elder council made an announcement about my promotion, but no one stepped forward to congratulate me. Ashwin stood at my side, and Heva hovered at the edge of the crowd, her eyes wet with pride. That was enough for me.

Then I looked over the crowd, and there was Eusebia, watching me carefully. When my eyes met hers, she smiled and nodded once. She was here for me as well.

That was more than enough.

Chapter Twenty-Six

My first run as leader was quick in coming. Osuin and Helm were to go out with me and Ashwin. Another pair, two women named Silvan and Rhea, a handspan of years older than me were also meant to come along, but at the last minute had to back out. A fierce storm had kicked up the night before we left, and a tree had fallen on Rhea's home, damaging it significantly. There were others to do the work of fixing it, but she wanted to stay and oversee it herself. We decided to go without them.

Secretly, I was a bit relieved that they wouldn't be on this particular run. They were both strong and competent, I had no complaint concerning their skills. However, both were long married to miners, and when they thought they were out of earshot, they spoke so frankly about the business of marriage, it made my miserable ears burn. I had never hated having good hearing quite so much as when Silvan and Rhea were in a mood to gossip about their loving husbands.

Still, two experienced runners were not a lot for accompanying two green ones.

"What are we going to do with these boys if we meet a breacher?" I asked Ashwin the day before we set out.

"Between us, we have nine stripes," Ashwin answered with his usual frankness. "If we meet a breacher, we kill it."

That was that.

I started the morning with my nerves jangling like a breacher was already breathing down my neck. Osuin was feeling very sure of himself from the great height of a single run. Helm was less impressed by his brother's single run, but he looked at me with wide eyes that made me a little shivery in the guts.

"We're going a long way, boys," I said as we passed the camp's outer boundary. This was the farthest from home that Helm had ever been. "We'll take it in easy stages. We're a small group, so we'll be quick enough. If everyone pulls their weight, we'll be just fine."

Helm nodded, and Osuin grinned. Ashwin followed behind, his head tilted back as if he weren't listening. It would be an error to think he wasn't.

The first day out was peaceful, the kind of day every runner wished for. The boys did what they should, the horses were in high spirits, even Ashwin was in a good mood, chatting with Helm about some finer points of woodcraft.

I tucked into my bedroll that night with an easing of the tension in my chest and shoulders. Maybe I could do this after all.

The next day, Helm's horse threw a shoe, and I wondered if we should turn around and go home. We could start over in a day or two. The boys were crestfallen at the mere suggestion.

"There's always that village, the one off trail a bit?" Ashwin said. "We can walk that far to give his horse a break."

Osuin had turned eighteen while we were back at camp, and Helm was now seventeen. They were my same height, so when I spoke to them, it was eye to eye. Yet I still felt as if I were looking down at them from a ledge. Their inexperience and youth shined out from their faces, it made me feel old.

"Ashwin's right," I told them. "There is a downlander village another two days from here. If we go easy, we can get Helm's horse shod there."

"Downlanders?" Helm asked, his eyebrows raising. "Just two days away? I didn't think any of them were that close."

"Four days from Iron Camp," I corrected. "It's a small settlement, and a new one. They set up there maybe seven years ago. They do us a good trade in linen."

"What's the place called?" Osuin asked, sounding miffed to not already have this information under his belt. "Why didn't we go there last time?"

"As far as I know, it doesn't have a name," I answered. "And we didn't go last time because no one needed their horse reshod a day out of camp."

Helm colored, but it wasn't his fault. Horses lost shoes sometimes. We set our noses eastward, and started walking.

Helm was complaining loudly about the wear on his travel moccasins when, two days later, the trees cleared enough to show the village. It was a quiet place, little more than a single row of buildings ending at a church. A smithy was set up midway along the path, and I paused before heading toward it.

"Boys," I said, turning to them. "I know you've not met downlanders before. Be polite. Don't give them a reason to hate us. We won't linger here, but it's best to leave on good terms."

Osuin and Helm nodded quickly, their eyes wide but their mouths set.

"I could wait here with the boys, if you'd rather," Ashwin added from the rear of the group.

"No. It's good experience for them to set foot in a downlander village. This won't be the last one if they plan to continue as runners. Might not even be the last one on *this* run."

I clicked to Obadiah and we started walking again.

There were a few people on the path as we came into view. A woman with a basket on one arm and a child trailing behind stopped in the way, then turned and left as if we'd approached her with weapons in hand. I frowned, watching her flee.

An elderly man was standing on his porch, and he leaned out to gawk at us. I knew that Lightwalkers hadn't had a lot of dealings with this village, except the twice yearly trade off of linen, but this reaction seemed excessive.

"Pardon me," I called to the man leaning off of his porch. "Is there a blacksmith here?"

Instead of answering, he hooked his thumb to his left, indicating a place farther up the path. I tipped my head to him and continued walking.

"You staying the night?" he called in a gruff voice.

"Depends. Can your smith shoe a horse for us today?"

The old man grunted, then went back into his house.

I kept moving, leading my three companions in a line down the path, and leaving plenty of room for others to pass us by.

No one passed.

Like an unspoken signal had been sent out, the people of the village began turning away from us, disappearing into their homes or the chapel at the end of the path.

"What's this about?" Osuin whispered behind me. I gestured at him to stop talking, but over his head I glanced at Ashwin.

Not good, not good.

Don't be afraid. You're about to meet someone.

I hope whoever it is doesn't run off at the sight of us. The Voice, however, had no more to say.

We quickly arrived at the blacksmith's place, a building with one side completely open. A big forge heated the air around it unbearably warm. I tugged at my bandana.

"Ho there!" I called. There were the sounds you'd expect from a blacksmith, hammer blows and the whoosh of hot metal hissing in oil. A large man was smacking a plowhead out on an anvil, swinging a hammer larger than my arm. At his side was a skinny youth, not much different than the two following me, working a bellows. A third man was standing in front of them, gesticulating wildly.

This third man was old enough to be my father, unless I was off the mark, but moved and spoke with the energy of someone half that age. He was a small man, with a wiry build, and a canvas satchel hooked over one shoulder.

At my call, all three looked up. The blacksmith's face darkened, the boy's went pale, but the third's looked intrigued.

That'll be the one to talk to, I thought. I looked him over as he looked over me in turn.

"I'm looking to get a horse shod. Is that something you can do here?" I asked, keeping my voice friendly and neutral. It wasn't easy speaking so calmly to people who were openly suspicious. For a second time, I wondered if we shouldn't have just gone back home and had done with it. What on the land was I going to do if these villagers turned hostile?

"You going to answer the man or not?" the wiry third man asked, looking over his shoulder at the smith. "I certainly can't do it."

"You know what the new priest says about them Lightwalkers!" the smith answered with a hiss.

"Oh pishposh!" the third man snapped, his face scrunching up in disapproval. "Brother Panuel never had a problem with 'em, and truth be told neither did none of us until this upstart showed up in the village! I say give the man a horseshoe so he can be about his business. Then we can be about ours!"

"Not sure as I want you to be about your business, Hemlock," the smith exclaimed, his hand going to his jaw.

"That tooth ain't going to start hurting less from waiting. I'm going to pull it. Whether I have to knock you out before or not remains to be seen!"

The youth was looking between the men, hands wringing with nerves.

"Well, you heard Hemlock," the smith said, jerking his head toward the youth. "Get up a shoe for that horse and let's be done with it."

The youth went white as a sheet, and looked at me with eyes wide enough to take in the world.

"I mean you no harm, boy," I said easily. Then turned to point out Helm. "It's his horse that needs attention."

Helm nodded to the youth sidling up to him.

"I'll need to size the horse's hoof first," he said quietly. Without answering, Helm ran a hand down his horse's leg, and got her to lift her foot for inspection. The boy took a stick out of his pocket and made a mark with a bit of charcoal. Then he scurried away to rummage through a bin for a promising shoe.

"Don't see the likes of your kind around here much these days," Hemlock said, speaking to me the way he had to the other man. Here was one who was not afraid of Lightwalkers. Some of the tension bled out of me.

"Not a lot of reason to head due east from our camp, to tell the truth. We mostly go south these days."

"I know you still trade for the linen," Hemlock said, nodding his agreement. "We still appreciate that, never you mind what they were saying before."

"I noticed the change in attitude. What's happened here?" I asked, though I knew the answer. I'd heard enough to draw a conclusion already.

"We've always had a white-robed or brown-robed priest here. They don't mind your kind, certainly don't make a big fuss out of it. This fella' we just got though, he minds. Can't say I approve, to be honest with you, stranger. That trade in linen props up a lot of people here."

"We also rely on the linen we get here. I'd hate to think the relationship had soured," I answered honestly. Half of us were wearing linen from this village right now. We would be forced to travel much further afield to replace it.

"I don't know how Lightwalkers run their place, a mayor or sheriff or what," Hemlock said, eyeing the boy pounding a shoe in place. "But you might let whoever know that things are changing here. They might want to come have a say in that. I know nothing I say has made a whit of difference. Might listen to the biggest source of income in the village though."

I suppose this is who I was supposed to meet? I'll have to tell the elder council.

This is part of the reason.

There's more? Should I stay longer?

No. That's all for now. But don't forget this moment.

I looked over the wiry man in front of me. I couldn't imagine needing to remember such a simple conversation for longer than it took me to relay it to the village council. Regardless, The Voice had led me true all of my life. I committed his face to memory.

"What is it you do here, sir?" I asked. The man had been watching the shoe go on, and he looked at me as if he'd forgotten I was standing there.

"Village bonesetter."

"Bonesetter?" I asked. What a title!

"Eh...your kind call us healers."

Hemlock, village healer. I'd do my level best to remember him.

Chapter Twenty-Seven

Our path was already thrown off by the change in direction so early in our trip. We could easily recount our steps and start again, but instead I decided to take us through a more heavily populated route. We could follow the big river south, passing through every town and city that the downlands supported. It would be a slower trip, but after our encounter in the little no-name village, I was itchy to know if the same changes were happening elsewhere.

"Didn't much like how that went," Ashwin told me the next day.

"Me, either," I answered. We were riding side-by-side on a wide part of the trail. We'd sent the boys ahead a few paces to scout. I was fairly certain they would find nothing, but there was no training without doing. And there was no doing without risk. I kept an ear cocked for any scuffle that might signal something amiss.

"You're wound up, Cunigast," Ashwin said. I looked over, expecting it to be a jest, but he was as serious as usual.

"My first run as the lead, two inexperienced runners who also happen to be my kin. I suppose I have a reason."

"You do. Won't help though. You're better when you're relaxed. Seen it a hundred times."

"What have you seen a hundred times?" I asked, still expecting a joke to be lurking under his commentary.

"Seen you spot a breacher a league before anyone else, when you were thinking about something else. Gathering wool, you call it. It's like that's when you're really the sharpest. It's...odd."

I took a moment to appreciate the irony of Ashwin calling me odd.

He made a valid point though. Most runners spent years training themselves into a kind of keen awareness. I had never bothered. Yet I sported more stripes than anyone in camp. It *was* odd.

"What would you have me do, Ashwin? They are my sister's children," I asked, dropping the reins to spread my hands wide.

"Relax. Trust your instincts," Ashwin answered. "And mine."

"I trust your instincts with my life."

"And theirs?"

I clapped his shoulder. "With theirs too, or you wouldn't still be my partner."

"Like you could get another," Ashwin said, but this time it was a jest. He was grinning from ear to ear.

The boys came racing back up the path.

"What did you find?" I asked, debating between laughing at them and reprimanding them. They were noisy enough to scare off anything nearby.

"Nothing," Osuin answered for them both, pulling his horse up short. "Not a blighted thing!"

"That's good news, boy!" I answered, a huff of laughter at his exasperation. "That's the best news!"

"I was hoping you'd sent me out because you knew something would be there!" Osuin answered. I saw the grimace, and understood.

"I'm not coddling you," I said evenly. "This is all part of the training."

"Doing nothing is training?" he snapped, then seemed to regret it. He jerked his horse around and pushed further down the path.

"Don't mind him, Uncle Cunigast," Helm said, apologizing for his brother's snappy attitude. "He's just frustrated he hasn't gotten a stripe yet."

"It's only his second run!" I exclaimed.

"You got yours on your first, didn't you?" Helm asked. I blinked at him, mouth agape.

"Is that what you boys were hoping for? A stripe on your first run?"

Helm blanched, but managed to stammer an answer out.

"We were hoping to be like you."

The silence filled my ears like a rushing wind.

"Go catch your brother, Helm," Ashwin said. He waited for Helm to disappear down the trail then turned toward me.

"Still think you aren't worthy of the command?" Ashwin asked.

"Yes!" I answered honestly. "This only makes me feel less worthy. Those boys think I'm some legend to live up to, but you know as well as I do that finding a breacher is more about luck than skill."

"Not killing them," Ashwin countered. "You must admit that there's skill involved in that."

"Skill we've all trained for from birth!"

"Not like you, Cunigast. I saw you drilling those boys. I know I come from a different camp, but you are like nothing I've seen. I doubt you're normal in Iron Camp, either."

I dropped the reins to rub at my face. Is that what he really thought? Is that what they *all* thought? Gods Above, I was the least of them.

Who told you that?

Everyone I've ever known!

No, child. I never told you that.

I had no words for that either.

Ashwin patted my shoulder.

"We better catch up to them, or they'll really think they've made you mad."

"I'm not mad. I'm *shocked*."

"I doubt they know the difference."

Chapter Twenty-Eight

Osuin and Helm seemed to redouble their efforts. Ashwin and I were almost ornamental when it came to breaking camp in the morning, the boys were so diligent. More than once, Ashwin met my eyes over their bent backs and raised an eyebrow. The look meant, *See? Look how they try to earn your approval!*

Of all the things I had anticipated on this first run as leader, this had not even made the list.

Two days later, we started encountering downlander villages. The wide river was fat and lazy here, and while there was plenty of room for the flat boats that the downlanders seemed to favor, few people bothered to come this far north. The little villages were anemic, the villagers suspicious. I was surprised by our reception. I was accustomed to a friendly greeting from a round priest in a white or brown robe upon entering any downlander villager I encountered. The others might not speak to us, but more than once I'd found myself followed by curious downlander eyes.

"Is this how it always is?" Helm asked after we left another suspicious village.

"Never, in fact," I answered. "I don't know what is going on."

"We should find out," Ashwin said from his position in the rear.

"I intend to," I said, and started looking for another path.

Years ago, I'd helped return a girl to a village far to the west of the normal settlements. We were far enough south that if we cut directly west, we could find that village in about three days. If there was any luck in the world, that same priest would be there and remember me. Or better yet, the girl herself.

Three days later, I guided two very dirty boys and Ashwin through the thick woods and found the deer path that led to the village. It was a scanty place, more of a collection of ramshackle hunting lodges with a wooden chapel that had seen better days at the end of a narrow trail. I led the others around the edge of it, and they each pulled up close to me.

"What is this place?" Ashwin asked.

I told him the story of the girl I'd rescued on my first run. Helm and Osuin's eyebrows raised higher and higher as the story continued. Helm whistled long and low at the end. Ashwin, however, watched me as if he'd just discovered a frog under a rock.

"You think she might still be here?" he asked.

"I have no idea," I answered. "I don't even remember the girl's name. I was hoping the priest would still be here though."

"Do you remember his name?"

"Of course not," I answered. "I was just hoping I left an impression."

Ashwin's mouth quirked up in a grin. "You do that everywhere you go, Cunigast."

I ignored that comment entirely. We were close to the chapel, and I dismounted, leading Obadiah along and looping his reins around a post out front.

No one came out to greet us, but that sometimes happened. I stepped up and rapped my knuckles against the double doors. There were no windows set in the door or the front face of the chapel, so I stepped back and waited.

I didn't wait long. Soon a face was poking out from between the doors. Older, with weaker eyes, and looser skin around the jaws, but still the same person and the same white robes.

Thank the Gods Above!

"Hello," I said. "I don't know if you recognize me, but I passed through here years ago, and left a young girl in your custody."

The man squinted at me, then over my shoulder at the three other Lightwalkers on the lawn.

"Oh I remember you, alright," he said. "Left a king's ransom in iron bear traps for poor Bettina to start her life over again."

"Was it enough?" I asked. I'd often wondered what happened to her.

"Yes," he said. "And no."

I frowned.

"Better come inside," the priest said. He pushed the door further open. "Them, too, if they want."

It wasn't exactly the warm welcome I'd received so many years ago, but here was a chance to get some answers. I looked at the other three. They tied up their horses next to mine, and all four of us slipped inside.

The chapel was dark, and full of old wooden chairs, none of which I would have trusted with my weight. The priest was shuffling through another door at the opposite end of the large room.

"This way," he said, waving us over. "I have a room over here. We can have a cup of tea like civilized people."

I grinned. Downlanders had an interesting concept of civilization from the view of a Lightwalker, but I understood him. He was being hospitable.

"Remember your manners, boys," I whispered to Osuin and Helm. "Your mother will have your hide if I tell her you were rude to this man."

Spines suitably straightened, they marched behind me in silence.

The room in question was smaller than I had expected. There was a little metal stove in one corner and the priest heated a metal tea pot on its flat surface. I realized there was wood burning inside of it.

"I've never seen a stove so small!" I said.

"Ah yes," he said, setting an item of glass and wire over his nose. He looked through them, and his eyes looked larger. "A new thing out of Othnio. Most efficient for a little place like mine. Keeps me warm all winter long, but takes less wood than a fireplace."

Ashwin and I looked the thing over, noting its construction.

"And those?" I asked, leaning toward him to look at the glass circles balanced over his nose. "What do they do?"

The priest's eyes blinked. "Spectacles."

"They help you see?" I asked.

"Quite a lot! I thank the God on the Land every day for their invention!" He took them off and handed them to me. I looked through and saw that everything was made larger by the glass. The boys edged closer, and I turned so they could look as well.

"What is it for?" Helm asked.

"As people age, they often lose some of their vision. This helps them get a bit of it back," The priest answered.

I passed them back to the priest and he gestured for us to sit around his small wooden table. These chairs weren't much better than the ones in the larger room, but when we sat, they only groaned and did not break.

"What brings you back here, if you don't mind me asking, Lightwalker?" the priest asked. He poured tea for each of us, and we all nodded our thanks.

I'd encountered this often. Downlanders didn't try to learn our names, instead calling us all "Lightwalker" as if it were a title or a name itself. I didn't mind. I referred to them just as neutrally.

"I had a few questions that only a downlander could answer. I was hoping that if you were still here, you might take my questions with kindness instead of suspicion."

"You came to call in a favor," the priest said with a snort. "Kindness has little to do with it, I'll wager."

"Do priests wager?" Ashwin asked.

"No, as a matter of fact," the priest answered, looking at my partner for the first time.

"What did you mean about the girl?" I asked. "Yes and no."

"Ah," the priest sat back in his chair. "It's a sad story, but I suppose you deserve to hear it, if anyone. She had enough money from the bear traps to marry, and use the money as a kind of dowry. It wouldn't have been traditional, but I was willing to stand in as a guardian until arrangements could be made. That's what I was trying to do, in fact. But a few weeks later, we realized she was pregnant."

An anger I'd thought long buried raised its ugly head.

"Those men I found her with!"

"Yes, the very same," he answered. "Well, after that, no one wanted to marry her. She was so young, she didn't have skills to earn her way in the world. I kept her here for a time, tried to teach her to read, do some accounting. I thought we could send the child away for adoption and maybe she could go somewhere new and start over. Again. But she wouldn't be parted with the child."

I sat back, my tea suddenly cold.

"She's still here, you know. She lives in a hut out in the woods with her son. He's rising ten now. She's a tanner. Hard work for such a little woman, but she does a good trade in leather."

"Still here!" I exclaimed. "There's hardly a village. I don't know how any of you survive this place! But a woman alone? Gods Above..."

"The stringent agreements with the Lightwalkers don't help," the priest answered coolly. "Some of the sentiment toward your people has really turned. Back when

Copper Camp was still operating, the Lightwalkers came and traded. That helped us offset the cost of the hunting and logging restrictions. But the Copper Camp was abandoned, and the trade dried up. It's been hard ever since."

"Copper Camp was abandoned thirty years ago."

"That's right," he said. He took off his spectacles and rubbed them clear on his robe. "I was stationed here early in my career, and I've been here ever since. The God on the Land seems to have formed me to shepherd this little out of the way place. No one else seems to remember us."

I was silent, my mind turning over his words like a bundle of thistles. I'd been here to deliver Bettina some ten years ago. Had things been strained then? The truth was that we hadn't taken the time to notice. We'd handed over the girl and left.

"Is that why folks are so suspicious of Lightwalkers?" I asked.

"Here?"

"Everywhere," I said. "We've ridden down from Iron Camp by way of the river, and every town seemed unwilling to deal with us."

"I still correspond with some of my colleagues back in Othnio. I think I recall something about it. Let me see..."

He rose from his place and began rummaging in a desk drawer. Papers filled the little drawer. After a few moments, he pulled one free of the pile and brought it to the table.

"Ah, yes. Here," he said, squinting through his spectacles at the paper. "My old friend Horatio... well, you won't care about that. Let me read this part though.

"We are receiving new training regarding the wild men of the mountains we call the Lightwalkers. I have never had dealings with them myself, not like you, my friend. I had never had a reason to regard them as anything but an industrious people, maybe mysterious, but hardly a threat. Do you remember a fellow we were in school with, Hathas? He has been preaching against the Lightwalkers for years. Most of us have ignored him entirely. He had some bad business with them a long time ago, and I always chalked it up to a personal grudge. Not good for a holy man. However, recently, his teachings are catching fire. I've heard more than one priest speaking with Hathas's words this last year. I think it is only a matter of time until they spread wider than Othnio, into the wider world."

The priest raised his head to look at me.

"Hathas? I've never heard of him," I frowned.

"Nor I," the priest said, laying the paper aside. "Not that it matters. The point is that he's likely the reason you're having trouble in the towns."

I leaned back in my chair, a heavy sigh on my lips. The chair creaked ominously, and I straightened again.

"We need to carry this news back to the elders," Ashwin said, his eyes clear and level.

"Yes, we do," I said, then turned to the priest. "I thank you for the information."

The priest nodded, then sipped more of his tea.

"I know you Lightwalkers tend to sleep in the open, but we've a place you could bed down for the night if you've a mind to it."

I raised an eyebrow. "Where might that be?" I was thinking of the rickety chairs in the chapel.

"Bettina's place, actually. Thought you might like to speak to her again. She has outbuildings she's set up for travellers, to earn a bit of extra coin. Her boy helps her keep it up. Not too bad, truth be told."

I looked over at Ashwin and the boys. Could they tolerate that much contact with downlanders? I sighed again. I had failed that girl, all those years ago. I left her here with no one to speak for her. I doubt I could have done better than this priest, but guilt was not a logical beast, and it rode me. "We'll go see her, then."

Chapter Twenty-Nine

There was a thick row of hawthorns that marked the edge of Bettina's place. The rising smell of animal and leather was only somewhat dampened by the haze of the plant in full flower. To be honest, I'd prefer the smell of leather over the hawthorn bush.

The priest had given us clear directions but declined to escort us. I swallowed against a wave of anxiety at the idea of approaching this woman. Would she remember me? Would it be better if she didn't?

Gods Above, what if she screams? I remembered with painful clarity when she'd done just that as a girl.

"The priest said she takes in all kinds as long as they pay," Ashwin said at my shoulder. I looked at him, blinking. He shrugged. "You seem nervous."

I glanced back at Osuin and Helm straggling behind us, suppressing a string of swear words that would turn their ears inside out.

"I doubt they've noticed," Ashwin said with a chuckle.

"After what happened," I started, licking dry lips. "The women took care of Bettina, and I went back to deal with the horses. When I stepped back into camp, she screamed."

I ran a hand through my hair, hesitating at the edge of the row of hawthorn bushes. "What if she screams when she sees me?"

Ashwin shrugged again. "Then we'll leave."

Kicking myself, I led Obadiah around the final bush, coming into full view of Bettina's home. It was a simple place like every other building in this village. Wooden boards nailed up and neat rows of wooden shingles on the roof were the entirety of the construction. A stiff breeze would rattle it.

Racks for stretching skins were in the yard and under a sturdy lean-to were the benches and beams and vats that all tanners used for the working of their goods. A row of extra buildings were lined up neatly behind the little house, all smaller sisters to it.

It was neat, orderly and sparse. There was a pillar of smoke coming out of the main house, and I wondered if they owned one of those little wood stoves like the priest.

I was aware of Ashwin and the others bunching up behind me. We were walking our horses, and they were already beginning to browse in the little yard.

"I'll go knock on the door," I said, looking at Ashwin. He nodded, already forgetting my nerves in favor of looking over his horse. Not that I blamed him. I'd be much the same if the roles were reversed.

Halfway toward the house, I realized this entire scenario would be different if I'd saved a lad all those years ago.

Am I ever to learn how to speak to a woman? I raised my hand and knocked before I could talk myself out of it.

There was a rustle, then the door opened, revealing a skinny boy with a mop of brown hair. He rose to the center of my chest, but it was clear he was far from done growing.

"Hello," he said, squinting up at me. "You here for leather or a place to stay?"

I tried smiling, "A place to stay, if your mother agrees to it."

He shrugged. "Don't know why she wouldn't, unless you can't pay. Do you got money, mister?" He was squinting again.

"I have money, boy."

"Well, wait here then." He shut the door, and I could hear him yelling on the other side, "MA!"

A few moments later, I heard footsteps coming. The door swung open again, and there was the girl, all grown up.

Well, grown. Not much up. She was a short woman. She looked up at me, just as squinty as her son. Quickly her eyes cleared, her mouth opening to a small 'O'.

"I don't know if you remember me," I started. Her hand was at her mouth though, her other at her stomach.

"Of course I remember you," she said, her voice shaky. "You saved my life."

The boy was looking between us. Then his brow cleared.

"Oh," he said, sounding unimpressed. "You're *that* Lightwalker."

Chapter Thirty

Bettina tried to give us the room for free, but I couldn't agree to that. I paid her what she asked, and decided I would leave more money on my cot in the guesthouse.

Her son, whose name was Hawthorne of all things, built up fires in our rooms and brought us each clean blankets and towels. Then, he drew water by the bucketful and heated it on the stove so we could each have a bath in the big copper tub she kept out back for just that purpose. It was luxury beyond belief to four men on the trail.

Bettina cooked up a big pot of stew that was generously portioned with meat, likely a benefit of staying with a tanner. She gathered us around the table like coins in her pocket and doled out the stew with a practiced hand.

I had no idea what to say to Bettina. I caught her looking at me across the table, her mouth open as if to say something, but no words ever came out. Hawthorne, on the other hand, sat at my elbow, asking questions like I held the strings to the world.

"How far away is Iron Camp from here?" he asked, the most recent in a line of questions about Lightwalker life.

"If you rode straight through the woods, it'd take you a week to get there, I suppose. Unless the weather was bad," I answered without much thought. Osuin and Helm were eating their fill, their eyes wide and blinking like cows in a new field.

"Oh yeah," Hawthorne said, nodding his head. "Got to think about the weather."

I suppressed a chuckle.

"Do you ever get up to Othnio?" he asked.

"Hawthorne!" Bettina snapped with a warning tone. I looked between them. Hawthorne was ducking his head in a way that let me know this was part of some larger argument between them.

"Not too often," I answered neutrally. "We try to avoid the bigger cities when I make the trip. Some of the other Lightwalkers like it there though and go through every time."

"So there'd be Lightwalkers there, if I were to go?" Hawthorne hazarded the question, wary eyes on his mother.

"I suppose so. Never a lot of us in one place that isn't a camp though."

Hawthorne was nodding again, but behind his eyes, I could see the wheels turning. I wondered what that was about. Bettina was frowning into her stew. Whatever it was, it wasn't my business.

After the meal, we went back to our guesthouse, which was just another thin-walled building with a dirt floor. Still, it was swept clean and full of fresh rushes. There was a fatter, older version of the stove the priest had squatting in a corner and it filled the room with a heat that would likely leave me running outside in the night just to cool off. We were each given a bed with freshly laundered blankets.

Osuin sat down hard on his bed and started peeling off his shoes the moment we were left alone.

"What do you think that was about, when the boy asked you about Othnio?" Helm asked. He took the bed beside his brother and began unlacing his own tall moccasins.

"Not our business," I answered.

"Yes, sir."

I stepped out, headed for the outhouse. Hawthorne was outside, his back to our guesthouse, head tilted back to look up at the darkening sky. He heard the door behind shut and startled, then ducked his head.

"Sorry," I said. "Didn't mean to sneak up on you."

"S' alright," he answered. "Just got my head in the sky again."

I stepped up beside him, taking in the sky.

"I don't want to live here for the rest of my life," Hawthorne said.

"Then don't," I answered. I chided myself. This wasn't my business. Hadn't I just told Helm that?

"Ma wants me to stay and take over her leatherworking business. She doesn't want me to leave her."

"Beg pardon, but why does *she* want to stay here?" I asked. I'd been surprised to find her still here.

"Scared to leave, I s'pose," he answered, shrugging. It was a dismissal that belied his youth. A ten-year-old boy who'd lived a cozy life tucked away from the world with his mother couldn't understand being afraid of anything. Nothing except not mattering in the world, maybe.

"Don't judge her too harshly," I said. "She's probably got her reasons."

"I'm a man though," he answered, puffing his chest out. Then, just as quickly, he deflated. "Or I will be. Can't see that I'll be much of anything if I just stay here, hiding behind her skirts."

"Is that what you think you're doing?" I asked, putting a bit of iron in my voice.

"What else?" he asked. I could hear his frustration. More hubris, more youthfulness.

"Boy, you're not hiding behind her skirts. You're taking care of her. She's alone in the world except for you. She's worked hard to raise you up and give you a good life. Now a real man would turn around and make sure she's taken care of from now on. Don't leave her alone after all that hard work. A man takes care of the people who need him."

Hawthorne's eyes got squinty, staring off at the sky again.

"Is that what you did, sir?" he asked. My throat went dry.

"As much as I've been able," I answered. It was as honest as I could be.

Chapter Thirty-One

The next day, Bettina stood in the yard and watched us leave. I said my goodbyes, tipped my head in her direction, and rode out.

Gods Above, what else could I do for such as them?

Don't worry about those two. I've got other plans for them.

It was still another day of riding before the imagined weight of responsibility for Bettina and Hawthorne were fully off of my shoulders.

"What now, Uncle Cunigast?" Osuin asked. He rode a broad-chested horse that would likely be just as happy pulling a plow at a downlander farmstead.

"As to that," I said, turning to look at Ashwin. As usual, he was looking up at the sky, appearing for all the world like he wasn't listening at all. "I was thinking of turning back. We have news to share. We could make a good sweep through the uninhabited forest between here and there and make a good accounting of ourselves."

"I thought we were meant to go to the ocean?" Helm asked. I heard the disappointment.

"Do you think you'll want to continue going on runs?"
I asked him. "Or would you rather, after your experience so
far, settle in the camps and work? There's no shame in either
path. You'll be asked to decide once we get back."

It was a relevant question. If this was his one and only
run, it would be his one chance to see the ocean and the
mysteries beyond. But if he was going to continue, there
would be more chances.

Helm's eyes slid toward his brother. They both sat up
straighter in the saddle.

"I want to be a runner, Uncle Cunigast. Like you. Like
Ashwin."

Our horses were walking along beside each other. I
leaned over and gripped his shoulder.

"Good man. Heva will be proud," I answered. It was
true. She would be scared every day he was out of sight, but
proud.

"Helm and I want to stay light partners," Osuin said,
pulling his own horse up on the other side of Helm's. "And
we want to go on runs with you, if you'll have us."

"There are other leaders," I said, quickly. "You should go on a few runs with others before you decide to stick with me. It'll be good experience, and I value that."

They looked between each other, and nodded toward me.

"If that's what you want, we'll do it," Helm said. "But we already know we want to work with you. We decided that a long time ago."

"Because of your mother?" I asked. "I won't be easier on you because you're family, you know."

"I think you've proved that!" Helm exclaimed, and Osuin gouged him hard in the ribs.

"You have the most stripes of anyone in Iron Camp," Osuin added. "Da talks with some of the traders from other camps, and he says you might have the most stripes in all the camps."

I hadn't heard that before. And from Roderic, of all people?

"I wouldn't know about that," I said. "Besides, Ashwin has almost as many."

"And he's your light partner," Helm said. "That's just more reason to want to go with the two of you on runs."

"Well, as it stands, you *are* my family, and I *do* want you. You'll both grow to be good runners, unless I've missed my mark. But don't expect me to ease up on you. You'll always have to prove your worth and pull your weight. Start getting lazy on the trail and you're out!"

Both boys straightened up and delivered a salute.

"Now, enough of that," I said, dismissing the formality of the moment. Or maybe the emotion. "Both of you scout ahead and tell me how you find the trail. We're going to cut directly north. There should be a little deer path in another couple of paces that turns our way. Go find it."

Boys and horses sprang away, equally high-spirited. The moment they were out of sight, I slumped in the saddle.

"What's this? Weighed down with all that hero worship?" Ashwin said, chuckling. His horse replaced Helm's beside me.

"What am I to do with them?" I asked, rubbing both hands down my face. "They are so blighted young, Ashwin."

"Train them, I reckon," he answered, leaning back in his saddle to look up at the clear sky again. Sun bathed his face, and he let a wave of light roll off of his skin.

"My sister's children," I said. "Gods Above, if something happens to them..."

"Don't go making trouble where there is none. They are both fine right now. Let's just deal with that."

"And that's enough. You're right," I answered.

"You know there will likely be others like them to come along?" Ashwin was giving me that fishy look he sometimes got.

"How do you mean?" I asked, as squinty as Hawthorne for a moment.

"Boys clamoring to go on runs with The Great Cunigast!" he said, holding his hands up as if my name were written in the sky. I rolled my eyes.

"I cannot believe that's true." I snorted. "They just feel like this because of Heva."

"You really believe that, don't you?" Ashwin said, frowning at me. He had that look again, like he'd turned over a rock and found a frog. I had surprised him, but I didn't know how.

"Don't you?" I asked.

"Laela thinks you're the greatest runner of our generation, and you know how she feels about *me*."

I stiffened at that.

"What?" I sputtered, actually sputtered, like a cow that's stepped too deep in a river.

"And you'll remember what I said about Tor and Lasha. Not that Lasha will admit to anything, but I overheard her talking to Tor about it once."

My face went to my hands, fingers rubbing my temples. A fierce ache was building up there.

"Ashwin, that's ridiculous! I'm the least of us." I groaned. "Stop. I cannot…"

My voice trailed off, but Ashwin put his hand on my shoulder. A trickle of light filtered into my skin and the headache washed out like water through a sieve.

"Cunigast, I don't know why you think you're the least of anyone. You're the best man I know."

I was spared the necessity of answering that impossible statement by the sound of hooves.

"We found it!" Helm shouted. He was followed quickly by his brother. Both of them had red flags of excitement on their cheeks, and their horses were breathing hard.

They probably galloped the whole way, silly boys, I thought. Then, *they trust me with their whole lives. Gods Above, save us all!*

I sucked some air into my lungs and put on a smile.

"Good job," I called. "Lead the way then. Ashwin and I will stay in the rear."

They turned their horses and started back the way they'd come. They each had the same skin coloring as me, and hair as dark as their mother's. Osuin had her tall frame and fine bones, but Helm was built as broad and sturdy as his horse. Without really noticing, I'd come to love them down to my bones. I thought about their wide-eyed adoration, and that heavy weight I'd felt standing in Bettina's yard resettled itself in the space between my shoulderblades.

Any advice? I asked The Voice.

There was only silence.

Chapter Thirty-Two

We returned from Helm's first run with no problems. I reported everything to the elder council, from the trouble with downlanders, the no-name settlement close to ours and the suspicions that it might fall on a new popular priest preaching against us in Othnio. They were rightfully concerned, but once I gave my report, my duties were done.

Eusebia's husband, a full decade older than either of us, was already on the elder council. I always exited as soon as was politely possible. His name was Pilan, and he followed me out of the council lodge. At first I thought he was only leaving at the same time I was.

"Cunigast, wait!" he called. I pulled up short and sucked in a breath.

"Yes, Pilan?" I asked, stopping on the step.

The council lodge was a large square building made of stone carried from the mine. The steps were wide and large. The rest of the council must be leaving because they came streaming out of the building and parted around us like we were just another rock.

"Can I ask a favor of you?" he asked, brow creased. He was a handspan taller than me, and wore his hair long and loose. At 41, it was entirely grey, and iron-colored to match the rocks around us. He'd been a horse trainer, amongst the best, before becoming an elder. Now he only trained a handful of horses. Ashwin's horse was one of his. Though I was well aware of who he was, I had never spoken to him.

"What is the favor?" I asked.

He looked around, noting the flood of bodies around us.

"Walk with me?" he asked. I followed him away from the square. As if without conscious decision, his feet turned toward the horse training corrals.

"I know you were a friend of Eusebia's," Pilan started. I felt my heartbeat pounding in my neck.

"Yes," I said. We arrived at the nearest corral, and Pilan leaned with his back to the rail. I gripped the rail in one hand, and focused on the tight contact between my fingers and the wood.

"We've had our children. I don't think we'll have any more," Pilan said.

What could this possibly have to do with me?

"Our oldest is ten now, old enough to watch over her other siblings. Eusebia has decided to return to running. She's been training herself up for months now."

My throat was dry, my eyes steady on the rail. *Eusebia on runs again? Surely he's not going to ask me...*

"Would you take her with you?" Pilan asked.

My heartbeat had been throbbing in my neck and now it was pounding between my ears.

"Has she requested this? Does she know you're asking me?" My eyes met his. He didn't flinch.

"No."

"I won't agree to it until she knows you've asked this. She might not prefer to go on runs with me, Pilan," I answered. It was the truth. I couldn't imagine going on a run with her in company, myself. I was likely to make mistakes if every time I looked up her honey-colored eyes were looking back. Gods Above, I was likely to get my whole company killed!

I started walking away, but Pilan spoke again.

"You're the best, Cunigast. I just want her to be safe."

I heard in his voice that he cared about her. I'd never been sure if that made it better or worse.

"I understand, Pilan. I really do. Talk to your wife though."

I didn't even look back to answer, just said it with my back to him. That said, I stalked off, a terrible headache forming behind my eyes.

Ashwin and Laela were still meeting in secret. I couldn't stop them. I was too much of a coward to tell his wife, or anyone else. Surely someone would discover them. Surely this couldn't go on forever. I dreaded the day it all came to light, as much as I feared it would never come.

Now that I'd heard those words from Pilan, I had my own troubles.

What will I do if Eusebia wants to go on runs with me?

What will I do if she doesn't?

The thoughts rolled around and around until I was sick to death of being inside my own head.

The headaches continued. Ashwin stopped by more often, just to help rid me of them. I told him what happened. I told him about Eusebia. I'd never told anyone. The words were clumsy and foreign in my mouth.

"You've stood by and watched her marry someone else, have children with someone else, all this time?" Ashwin asked.

"What choice did I have?" I asked. The misery was choking me, cutting off my air. If I stopped breathing, it would be a kindness.

Then I realized what he was really asking. I hadn't done what he and Laela were doing. I watched some of the light recede in Ashwin's eyes.

"No wonder you're so disapproving of us," Ashwin said softly.

I didn't know what to say. Words and feelings were choking me, but I pushed them all back. The worst thing I could do was cry in front of my light partner.

"Cunigast," Ashwin asked. "Can you share some light back to me?"

"What?" He'd never asked for light from me. From anyone. He clearly didn't need it.

"Just do it, please," he said, holding his arm out.

The truth was, I'd so rarely shared light, I was clumsy about it. I latched his arm to mine, and focused on the vibrant flow of light in my body. Slowly, but not slowly enough, I pushed some out of me and into Ashwin.

After a few seconds, Ashwin nodded, signaling that it was enough. I shut the link down and waited.

Ashwin swallowed, blinked, looked away.

"What is it?" I asked. "Did I share too much?"

"More than I expected," he said.

Ah. I'd shared my emotions, too. I winced.

"Learn anything useful?"

"I was right," he said, and stood to leave. He stretched his arms high above his head, then looked down at me with the small smile I'd become so familiar with over the years.

"Right about what?" I asked.

"You're the best man I know."

Chapter Thirty-Three

What discussion might have happened between Eusebia and Pilan, I never learned. Regardless, a month later Eusebia joined my group for a run.

Osuin and Helm had gone on three consecutive runs with whoever would take them, barely staying more than a day back in camp in between. Now, considering themselves thoroughly seasoned, they were determined to run with me and me alone. I conceded, though a scant two months of runs was hardly enough to consider anyone *experienced*.

I stood at the edge of Iron Camp, horse reins in my hand and looked. Osuin and Helm were coming forward, Ashwin not far behind. Eusebia followed, along with her sister-in-law, a sturdy woman named Ishik who had up until recently been staying home with children. The two women walked and talked easily, and it reminded me so strongly of that first run with Eusebia that my breath caught in my chest.

Pilan stood at the edge of the training field, watching her go. Eusebia turned to look back at him, raised a hand and waved. He waved back, and turned to walk away.

I'd have watched her all the way out, until I couldn't see her anymore.

Guilt swamped me. *No use in thinking that. She was never mine.*

Ashwin was glowing softly, and I reached out for a pull of light from him.

"Ready to go?" he asked, his eyes searching mine. I swallowed.

"Ready as I'll ever be."

"Say the word, and I'll take over. If you need me to," he said. It was a kind offer. I knew I'd never take it though. Gods Above help me.

"Ma packed us some bread for the road," Helm said, tugging out his bandana and tying it around his neck.

"It'll be bad two days out," I exclaimed. Most of the time a full loaf of bread was too large to justify taking on a long trip.

"I know. We'll have to eat it up tonight!" Helm said. He was laughing, always laughing.

"I stole a little jar of jelly," Osuin said, a little quieter but just as excited. "We can have it with the bread."

I smiled. These two would surely keep me sane.

"Hello, Cunigast," Eusebia said. She was pulling her horse alongside the others, a small smile on her lips.

"Hello," I answered.

Nope. Those two boys were a light to me, but nothing to the roaring flame that was Eusebia. Maybe I'd take Ashwin's offer after all.

"Hey there," Ishik said. She stuck her hand out to shake mine. We'd never formally met, but like everyone else in camp, we knew each other in passing. "Glad to be on a run with you, Cunigast."

"Glad to have you," I answered. It was the Gods Above's own truth. She was Pilan's sister. If there was anyone who would want Eusebia to stay away from me, it would be her.

"We're going east for a ways and crossing the river. We're going down the river on the wrong side. A few settlements have started on the east side, or so I'm told. It'll be a rough march, but we aren't going as far south as Othnio."

The others were circled around me, looking serious but ready. This was how it would likely be. I gave directions, they followed them without question. If I could keep my head, everything would be fine. *Gods Above, please let this be a boring run!*

"Let's go. I want to make good time these first few days. We'll slow down once we hit the river."

And that was that. We were leaving. Pilan might as well be a thousand leagues away.

Ashwin rode silently at my side. I sent Osuin to ride in the rear position. I pulled Helm aside and asked him to linger near the women.

"They haven't been on a run in a long time. I doubt they'll have any trouble, but just in case," I said. His shoulders squared, proud to be asked to do something. I imagined the job would be unnecessary, but it gave him something to do.

And it put some distance between me and Eusebia.

"How are you faring?" Ashwin asked. He pitched his voice low. There was no chance anyone would hear him.

"I don't know, Ashwin," I said. "Keep an eye on me, will you? If my calls are off, say so."

"Done," Ashwin answered, and I knew he would.

The knife that Heva had given me was in my saddlebag. I always carried it with me, even if not directly on my person. I took it out occasionally to oil it. I wanted it to be in good working order. I always told myself it was in case we ever needed a spare. The truth was that I carried it hoping what Heva had hoped all those years ago.

I thought about giving it to Ashwin all the time. He was a brother to me in more ways than one. Right now, he was watching out for me. His light sharing kept me alive. What more could I ask for?

Yet I held back. Whatever stood between me and Ashwin, giving him the knife would be another burden to carry. I couldn't do that to him.

Eusebia wasn't actually shedding light, but to my eyes she might as well have been. Wherever she was, I saw her out of my periphery like a beacon. I couldn't give the knife to her, of course. A married woman with a family? It would be beyond inappropriate. Still, my eyes kept finding her figure, tall and narrow atop her horse.

We reached the river in five days, pushing hard. We crossed at a narrow point and rested the horses for a day on the other side.

Osuin and Helm stripped down and went swimming, going a respectful distance downstream from the ladies. I could hear them laughing and splashing like pups, and it brought a smile to my lips.

"They remind me of mine," Ishik said. She didn't speak often, but I was beginning to like the woman. She had raised four boys, and they were all within a few years of going on their own first runs. "Wish I had half their energy."

"You and me both," Eusebia said, and I suppressed a chuckle. She'd shown no small amount of energy on the trail. If I'd had any doubts, they were gone.

Ashwin was up in a tree a stone's throw away from us. With a jolt, I realized my mistake. It was down to Ishik to save me from being alone with Eusebia. I thought about joining the boys, but it was still too early in the spring for me to face that cold river. I could always sit on the shore and watch over them.

I stood to do just that.

"What do you say, Ishik?" Eusebia asked, mischief in her voice. "Should we go for a swim ourselves? Show these little boys that the adults know how to have fun, too?"

Ishik was looking at her the way I imagined she'd looked at her own children many times.

"Gast will swim with us, won't you?" Eusebia said, turning those sparkling eyes on me. And just like that, I was transported to that first run more than a decade ago, just as tongue-tied and helpless as ever. I was eighteen again, totally at her mercy.

"Oh, if you must, you old heifer!" Ishik said with a laugh. Ishik and Eusebia stood to start peeling leather leg guards and moccasins off.

"I'll just see if Ashwin wants to swim, too," I muttered and started walking. I prayed that neither of them noticed my burning ears.

"Ashwin!" I whisper-yelled once inside the cover of trees. "Where are you?"

"Here!" he called. His voice filtered down through the branches. I looked up and saw him, a good seventy handspans above my head. The thought of that height made my head swim.

"Get down here! Quick!" I snapped at him. Pacing at the bottom of the tree, I tried to settle myself.

"What is it?" he asked, materializing beside me as quick as a squirrel.

"The women want to go swimming," I said.

"That hardly sounds like an emergency."

"With me. They want- Eusebia wants- to go swimming *with me!*" I knew I sounded absurd. It *wasn't* an emergency. Somehow all of my twenty-eight years had shrunk down until I was a child again, seeing a pretty girl for the first time.

"Alright, alright. I'll come out, too," Ashwin said, shooing me ahead of him. "Don't get your skirt in a twist."

I groaned.

"Should we get the boys?"

"As they are likely buck naked, no. I don't think so."

Ashwin laughed. "Stupid kids. Who'd think it was fun to get naked in this water?"

I wasn't in a laughing mood though. We stepped back into the clearing to find the women down to loose trousers and cotton shirts. Gear was stacked in orderly piles around our campfire, and they were discussing the best place to get in the water.

We'd settled ourselves on a nice pebbly bit of beach, where the water greeted the land at a gentle slope.

"It's better to just jump in all at once, Ishik," Eusebia was saying. *Dear Gods, where have I heard that before?*

"I'm not as young as I once was, thank you very much. I'd rather tiptoe in with some dignity!" Ishik retorted.

Eusebia turned and saw us walking out of the cover of trees. She smiled.

"Cunigast will jump in with me, won't you Cunigast?"

"I suppose," I answered, ducking my head. Ashwin thumped me on the back.

"Me, too," he said. "There's a rise farther upstream. Though one of us should go tell the boys where we are."

I looked at Ashwin, "I'll go."

"I'll go," Ishik said, waving me off. "Then I'll tiptoe in where I want."

"Those boys are probably stark naked," I warned.

"Nothing I haven't seen a million times. Sons, you know," she answered with a shrug.

"You're like to scare them half to death!" Eusebia laughed.

"It'll be good for them!" Ishik answered, and disappeared around a stand of bushes.

"Where's that rise?" Eusebia asked Ashwin. He nodded sideways and we followed him. It was little more than a plethron upstream of us. The river had cut deeply into a soft part of the earth where a tall tree leaned precariously over the water.

"We could jump from that branch!" Eusebia said, pointing.

"We should throw a rock in first," I said. "Make sure the water is deep enough."

"I'll do it," Ashwin said. He picked up a hefty stone, and began climbing the tree. A matter of moments later, the stone sank into the water with a satisfying *glug*.

"Let's go!" Eusebia said, and started climbing. Ashwin took her hand and tugged her upward. I followed behind, watching her ankles to make sure she didn't slip.

Ashwin eased out first, the branch bending under his weight, but not much. He nodded once, and jumped. As he touched the water, he shed light, and we watched his glow under the water like a ghost light. Fish scattered, light and man equally terrifying.

"That's a neat trick!" Eusebia said, her voice light with wonder. Ashwin's light was reflected on her face as she peered down.

Ashwin's head resurfaced and he grinned up.

"It's freezing!" he shouted. "Jump in!"

Ashwin is having a great time! The thought sounded surly even to me. I tried to loosen the tension in my shoulders. I was wound so tight, I'd likely drown.

"Come on, Gast," Eusebia said. She was holding a branch above her head, and she held her other hand out to me. "Let's jump together."

I knew my heart must be in my eyes, but it didn't matter. I edged closer, feeling the branch bow under my bare feet. I took her hand, feeling the contact like fire.

We jumped.

Fire and ice.

Eusebia shed light, scaring a new wave of fish under the water. No doubt, she was trying to mimic Ashwin's trick, but she shared a glimmer of that light with me. I felt a torrent of joy through that flash of light.

Joy from freedom. She was free as a bird in the sky or water rushing out of a mountain spring. It washed over me, hitting me as hard as a hammerfall.

She let go of my hand. We surfaced. My world had flipped upside down again.

Chapter Thirty-Four

As I lay on the pebbly beach, damp, cold and surly, I reflected that this was familiar. Eusebia was a slow death. Her presence was like a splinter under my skin, like an infection that had spread raging red across my flesh and throbbed until I was mad with it. The prolonged contact convinced me that I would die from it. If not this moment, then surely the next.

My muscles were loose from the swimming, and I was pleasantly tired. Helm had built up a fire that was warming me slowly. Soon, I'd have to move away from it. For now, my hair was still damp, and it felt good.

Ashwin and Ishik were chatting nicely. Osuin and Helm were sitting with their heads together, restitching a tear in the threading on Osuin's saddle. Eusebia lounged between them, participating in the conversation when it suited her.

I didn't know what any of them were discussing. I was facing the dark forest at our backs, listening. There was a deep silence that had caught my attention. Surely there should be birds or insects here. The sun was low, soon to disappear below the horizon. It was the time when the forest emptied of day creatures and filled with night ones. As shadow creatures only ever seemed to bother humans, the animals ignored them entirely. *Oh to be a bird!*

A tiny touch on my back diverted my attention. I turned to see that Ashwin had flicked a pebble at me.

"You're brooding," he said. He was coming to sit beside me, joining me in my vigil.

"Am I?" I asked, but I knew he was right. "I thought I was guarding."

"Enough ears here for that. Besides, we're all awake."

"Fine. I'm brooding." I answered, folding my arms across my knees.

"You'll spook Osuin and Helm like this. And Ishik has already noticed your moods. She'll be asking questions before long."

"Gods Above," I muttered. "It's like travelling with Heva."

Ashwin smirked. "I'd like to go on a run with Heva someday. She's probably excellent."

"If she's kept up her training, she'd run circles around us," I agreed. For the first time, I realized I was proud of my sister. I frowned. How long had that pride been there?

Always. You just haven't been paying attention.

Why do you never answer when I want you to? I thought, just as surly to The Voice as I was to Ashwin.

Silence.

I huffed.

There was no answer, but I had the distinct feeling that The Voice was...smiling?

I rubbed my face with my hands.

"How do you know if you're crazy?" I asked Ashwin. His eyebrows rose to his hairline.

"I gave up asking," he answered. "Didn't seem to matter what the answer was. I was always going to be a runner, crazy or not."

"I don't know if I can say the same," I said, and picked up my own pebble to toss into the forest. "I think you're the only reason I get to be a runner."

"I doubt that's true now," Ashwin answered, tossing a pebble to land next to mine.

I snorted in answer.

"You seem to be under a permanent delusion about your value to Iron Camp," Ashwin said. He was looking at me square now, his eyes catching some of the light from the fire. "I don't know how much clearer I can be, Cunigast. You are the best runner we have. No question. Maybe the best runner in a generation."

I looked away. "Low standards."

"Low opinion of yourself."

A pause. Then, "And if I am crazy?"

"You're the sanest person I know," Ashwin answered. Now he sounded as surly as I did. Had I offended him? Gods Above help me if I ostracized my own light partner.

I'd never told Ashwin about The Voice. I wondered if his answer would be the same if he knew. I wondered if *he* heard The Voice.

Ashwin held out his arm, and I gripped it against my own. He peeled off enough light for me to last clear through the next day. I pointed one finger out toward the darkness and fired a bolt of light. It darted forward, quick as a wink, lighting up the spaces between the trees like a mythical bird of light. There was nothing there, not even the swirling of shadow creatures.

"Time for bed," I said. "Wake me after your watch."

Ashwin nodded, but did not look away from the forest and the empty darkness there.

Chapter Thirty-Five

"You've been avoiding me."

I startled hard and looked to my right. Eusebia sat there, straight as a rod on her horse, her eyes demanding an answer.

We were two days south of that pebbly beach. I could still feel the echoes of her tiny glimmer of light in my veins, and it screamed through me like an eagle's cry.

"Why do you say that?" I tried.

"Don't do that. I know you've been avoiding me. I just don't know why," she said. Gods Above, who was in charge here?

I couldn't make that complaint truthfully though. Eusebia had followed every order, and all six of us had worked together like a well-oiled downlander machine. We were a team made from the stuff of legends, and if it weren't for this one troublesome personal connection, I would beg the others to travel with me on every run.

Blight the woman.

"Do you really not know?" I asked, miserable. She blanched. So she did know.

"It's been so many years," she said.

"I'm aware. Your and Pilan's children will be going on their own first runs in a few years."

They might have been our *children.* My heart was a traitor, and I slammed closed the door on the thought.

"I didn't have a choice, Cunigast," she said, biting off the words between her teeth.

"Neither did I."

Eusebia was silent.

"I'm not angry," I said. "It just..."

Why couldn't I say the words?

"It just still affects me. *You* still affect me, Eusebia." She met my eyes, and there was a wash of feelings there that I couldn't begin to pick apart. "I'm only a man, after all."

"You don't even know, do you?" she asked, and this time the emotion in her eyes was plain. She was angry.

Eusebia snapped the reins for her horse and left me behind in a trail of road dust.

I stared after her, flummoxed. Whatever she'd been talking about, I *didn't* know!

Know what?

Patience, boy.

I gritted my teeth. If it weren't for the bone-deep comfort I gained from hearing The Voice inside my head, I would have sworn it- sworn *him*- off years ago. Even now, annoyed, a trickle of peace ran through my veins as clear as fresh light.

Another horse came clip-clopping up beside mine. I expected it to be Ashwin with some mysterious comment, or Osuin giving me a report of the trail conditions ahead.

Instead it was Ishik with a sunny smile.

"Nice riding out here today, eh?" she said. I nodded. It was a beautiful day, the kind a runner prayed for. The sun was high in the sky, not a cloud in sight. Hot enough to be comfortable riding, but cold enough to welcome a fire in the evening.

"Eusebia come talk to you?" Ishik asked. I nearly squeaked like a mouse.

"Well, she was just here," I started. How on the land was I supposed to finish *that* sentence?

"Ah, so yes," Ishik answered. "I can tell by the way your eyes are popping out of your head."

I looked at her, blinking. I suddenly had a desire to fade into the forest like a ghost and never see any of these people again. Dying couldn't be *that* awful, could it?

"You think I married a man, raised four boys, and learned nothing about how men and women are with each other? My brother loves Eusebia, but it was always clear to me that she didn't choose him."

I rubbed a hand down my face.

"It wasn't until your last stripe was added that I realized it was you she was moon-eyed for."

"*Moon-eyed?*" I choked on the word. Ishik just shrugged.

"I've never seen a woman so keen to go back to running after raising her children. Nor seen one train so hard. She's been up before dawn every day for nine months training for this. Did you know that?"

I shook my head. "I had no idea."

"I suspect there's a lot you have no idea about," she said with a laugh.

I only stared at her.

"Oh you're a good runner, there's no doubt about that. You're even a good man, as far as I can tell. And believe me,

I've been looking into you," she said, laying a finger alongside her nose and winking. "But you've not a clue about women. That much is plain."

"Not enough opportunities, I suppose." I scratched the back of my neck, certain I was red from top to bottom with embarrassment. In a few sentences Ishik had managed to make me more uncomfortable than any other person in memory.

"Well, I'll not tolerate Eusebia betraying her marriage vows. They are oaths we swear and that's nothing to toss aside on a whim," Ishik said, as stern as if I were one of her sons about to make a terrible decision.

"I would never!" I choked out, shocked. "I mean, I couldn't! I-"

Ishik waved a hand, shushing me.

"Cunigast," she said. I was sure she was holding herself back from squeezing my arm or patting me like a child. "My point is, that while you wouldn't, Eusebia *would*."

I recoiled from her, shocked.

"I can't believe that."

"You're the only one, then," Ishik said. "Eusebia is the sister of my heart. But I've watched her over the years. She wants to be the best at everything. When she was young, she was trained the hardest at her runner skills. Then she got married and was determined to be the best at raising children. Now, she wants to be the best again. And to her, you are a part of that. You're the best. She wants you like a daybreaker wants a soul."

I saw white. The world washed out of color like a rock left to bleach under the hot sun. I felt like a fool, too stupid to realize what I was in the eyes of the world. I was seventeen watching my father's funeral brazier burn again, watching Eusebia watch me from under the eaves.

"I like you, Cunigast," Ishik said. This time she couldn't resist. She reached out and rested her hand against my arm. "More than that, I respect you. So listen to my warning. Don't let her play with you. Set her straight, send her on her way. Back to her husband. Where she belongs."

I didn't respond. Ishik, at some later moment, must have ridden away. I didn't know how long I rode through the forest silent and alone in my mind. The world might as well have gone up in fire, or sank to the bottom of the Endless Sea. I was unseeing of it all.

Chapter Thirty-Six

Eusebia tried to corner me another time, which I avoided as if she carried some irksome disease. I couldn't hold my thoughts in my head where she was concerned, and I was afraid of what I might say to her.

After another attempt to single me out, I went to Ashwin.

"Don't let me be alone with her, Ashwin," I whispered to him at the back end of the group. "Please!"

"Are you sure that's what you want me to do?" Ashwin asked. I knew that he wouldn't judge me no matter my actions, but he plainly didn't understand.

"Swear to me."

Ashwin nodded.

Not that it mattered. I had forgotten how determined Eusebia could be when she was in a mood. And a mood had definitely descended on her. She stared at me across the campfires in the evenings, and she stared holes in my back on the trail. What on the land did Osuin and Helm make of it? I tried my best to ignore it, ignore *her*. Ishik's warning rang in my head until I felt like a bell, echoing tolls.

I threw myself into training the boys. They'd gone on three runs with other leaders, and I quizzed them endlessly about what tips they had learned, what skills they were still learning, and what they had mastered.

Osuin and Helm were keen to learn my trick of passing through treetops to scout an area from overhead. To date, they were still louder than a kitchen full of hens on slaughter day, but they kept at it.

Ashwin could do it, and he helped me. The truth was that while Ashwin could be just as silent in the trees, and dared to go higher, I was the fastest. Together, we were an intimidating pair of trainers.

The boys had both gained weight and muscle at a surprising rate over the last two months. They were quickly turning from boys to men. Osuin used his lankier body to skim across much skinnier branches, but Helm had the strength to pull himself along by his hands for much longer even than I could. I marvelled at the runners they might be in another handful of years. My chest swelled with pride.

Another blue-sky day on the trails pressed down on us. We were another day out from our final stop before turning around for home. I was weary beyond my years with this particular run. I'd racked my brain trying to come up with an excuse to get Eusebia off of my runs permanently. I hadn't come up with a single complaint about her performance as a runner, and citing personal issues was likely to raise a lot of eyebrows, particularly with her husband. I'd thought about it until I wished I could take my head off and leave it somewhere on the trail.

I was in the lead, Ashwin trailing far behind to guard our rear and shed some extra light. He still maintained the illusion that his shares with me were all the extra light he had, and I'd long grown accustomed to assigning him watches alone to shed his true excess off. Osuin and Helm were chatting with Eusebia and Ishik midway between us. Ishik and Eusebia liked to give the boys pointers that only women and mothers could give, and the boys liked to remind the women of their woodcraft with an honest earnestness that only the young could get away with. It was an unexpected pairing, but I was impressed by the progress of all of them. Aside from my difficulties, even Ashwin was doing well with this mix of personalities.

I gritted my teeth again. The problem, the only problem, was me. Maybe I should speak to Eusebia after all. Clear up this issue and move on.

Ahead. Quickly.

I listened closely, trying to pick up any sound, but there was none. I stood in the saddle, reached up to a passing tree branch, and pulled myself into the forest canopy. My horse, long used to my ways, stopped on the trail. Obadiah would wait patiently until the rest joined. His empty saddle would signal to the others where I had gone.

Passing silent and quick through the tree boughs like a mountain cat on the prowl, I eased myself forward in search of whatever The Voice had alerted me to.

This had happened so many times, that others attributed me with a preternatural sense for danger. It wasn't true. Every time, The Voice had alerted me to the danger first. I was no more or less capable than any other runner with my length of experience, only luckier. Without The Voice, I would be the least of my peers. The knowledge rang in my head every time Ashwin insisted I was the best. It was a lie, a falsehood that I could not divest myself of, no matter how honest I led the rest of my life.

Cunigast the Liar.

No one would believe it, even if I told them.

I peered into a clearing five paces off the deer trail we were following. There was a family of wolves there, a male standing guard over a female and four pups. The pups were ambling around the clearing on clumsy limbs, taking little bites at dandelions and climbing over each other. The male's guard hair stiffened. He sensed me.

We would have passed far around them. Why bring me out here?

I searched around for some other danger, but there was nothing. Frowning, I slipped backward into the trees, leaving the little family in peace.

Before I could reach the rest of the group, I found Eusebia following my path. She was balanced on a tree branch, hands holding onto another above her head. She had passed so silently that I didn't know she was there until I saw her less than a stone's throw in front of me. When had she learned that trick?

Eusebia saw me, too. She didn't say anything. She was waiting for a signal that it was all clear.

I paused, watching her watch me. The panic receded. For the first time I imagined I saw her clearly.

Eusebia was still as beautiful as ever, but there was strain to her expression that I hadn't noticed before. She looked tired, almost ready to cry. I wondered why she'd decided to follow me when she could have been resting on her horse.

Instead of signaling to her, I slipped closer until we were sharing a branch, and sat. I gestured for her to sit beside me. She did so, moving carefully. There were small changes in her body from the years. She was still strong, still fit, but maybe softer in places. Her hips were a shade wider, and her shoulders, too. I knew what the last decade had done to me. What had it done to her?

"Done avoiding you," I whispered.

She didn't say anything at first. The silence was enjoyable. There were birds overhead, and the near-constant scampering of squirrels that always seemed to be present in a forest. I heard the wind blow through the trees above us but did not feel it. The sun glittered down like a swarm of bright butterflies, tiny points of warmth on my skin.

"I'm sorry," Eusebia said.

"What for?" I asked. She owed me nothing.

"I wanted to marry you, Cunigast," she said.

I heard the words, and felt a loosening in my chest. There was no panic, no fear, only a sigh of relief.

"My father wanted sons," Eusebia said. "He was angry til he died that I wasn't a son."

"I didn't know that."

"No one did," Eusebia said. Silence again. I knew something about disappointing a father.

But no, that wasn't right. I remembered my father's final words to me. I hadn't disappointed *him*. He'd disappointed *me*. There was a world of difference between the two.

"He arranged my marriage almost as soon as we moved to Iron Camp. He was on the elder council, just like Pilan. I never had another option. He married us off so that my husband could be the son he never got."

Silence again.

"I tried, Cunigast. I went to the elder council and begged them to break the engagement to Pilan. He was a decade older than me and I didn't love him." Eusebia was crying now, but her voice was strong. "I never loved him, really."

"He loves you," I said. It wasn't a question. As much as I might want to hate the man, it was plain that he cared about Eusebia.

"He's been very kind to me," she said. "He deserved better than me."

"I doubt he would agree with that," I whispered.

"I just needed you to know, Cunigast," she said, finally turning to face me. "I couldn't ask you to dishonor yourself with me. I'm married. My husband is most likely going to live a long time, and I have said my vows whether I wanted to or not. I couldn't stand the idea of you lessening yourself by seeing me in secret. You deserve better than that."

"I'm not sure I agree with you about that, either. No man is good enough for you, Eusebia."

Eusebia's eyes closed. Softly, I wiped a tear from her cheek and she leaned into my hand.

"I just needed you to know."

I realized that Ishik was wrong. Eusebia didn't need to be the best at anything. She just needed to be better than a son.

That night, after the others were asleep, I sat with my back to them, listening to the sounds of the forest.

A calm had descended on me with Eusebia's words that hadn't lifted. I could hear the others' soft breathing, and the calm night breezes through the trees. The moon loomed large in the sky, and I imagined I could reach out and touch it.

I still can't have her, I thought to The Voice. *Why do I feel so much better?*

You never wanted to *own* her, boy. You just wanted someone to choose you.

It rang with truth. Even a month ago, it would have been a bitter truth. Not now. I felt free as a bird in the sky. Free as Eusebia's light felt.

I stood and went to my pack. Inside was the knife that Heva had made me all those years ago. I took it out and tucked it into my belt. I could never marry Eusebia, and that was okay. But I loved her. She should have the knife.

I turned back to my night watch and saw a flicker of silver in the forest. I stood, watching and waiting.

The male wolf passed into view. He stood watching me, standing guard for his own little troop as they passed behind him in the darkness. I nodded toward him. He dipped his head and turned, melting back into the darkness.

Part Four

Chapter Thirty-Seven

On the final day of our outbound journey, we found a settlement. Rumors had reached us that downlanders were beginning to push over the river to start settling the eastern banks. While it was not a violation of the long-standing agreement between Lightwalkers and those first downlanders to settle here, it was a departure from custom. We had found no sign of these rumors until now.

There was little more than a single row of clapboard houses connected by a wide boardwalk, hardly enough to be called a "settlement." Lightwalkers had hunting camps bigger than this place.

I rode Obadiah at a steady pace, the others arrowing behind me on the path. There wasn't a road leading into the settlement, only a dirt path down to the riverbank. The forest around the settlement was well-coppiced and we could easily pass through the spaces under the old stand of willows there.

On the boardwalk stood a woman in a long dress that had seen better days. The dress might have once been a pale pink, but now it was merely brown, the hem almost black with mud from the river. Her hair was up in a pile on her head, and her lips were painted a bright red. She leaned against one of the buildings and watched us ride up with the disinterest of someone who'd long resigned herself to whatever life sent her, good or ill.

I stopped Obadiah, but didn't dismount.

"Good morning, ma'am," I said, nodding toward her. She looked me over and shrugged.

"Never seen a Lightwalker come to a place like this," she said. She looked over at the people behind me and shrugged. "Don't know what you're doing here, either. You got womanfolk with you."

I frowned, and the confusion must have been plain on my face. Her eyes lightened.

"Oh, you don't know, do you mister?" she asked, and straightened. "What *are* you doing here?"

"We heard there was a new settlement growing on the east side of the river. We just came to see it."

"A settlement?" she laughed. "Is that what they're saying?"

"Is it not true?" I asked, leaning across the pommel to give Obadiah a pat along his neck.

"I suppose it's true in a way," she said. "We came here because we got nowhere else to go."

"Who are you? You and your people, I mean?" I asked.

"Women. We are a group of women, and we settled here because we got no men to take care of us. Not a lot of good options for a woman."

Eusebia and Ishik pulled closer, and I was glad.

"Can you not work in the villages?" Eusebia asked.

The woman looked at Eusebia like she was a wild creature. To a downlander, I suppose she was.

"I don't know what it's like for you Lightwalkers, but downlander women can't do anything without a man. We can't own property. We can't open a business. We can't work, unless it's for a man. Most of the work the men would allow us isn't the kind of work a respectable woman wants."

Eusebia was growing angry, but Ishik nodded. She seemed to know what this woman spoke of.

"So you don't own this place you've built here?" I asked, gesturing to the row of buildings.

"No one owns this. And the law agreed to ignore us over here. Sometimes men come rowing across to try to buy our time. We send them back. Sometimes a woman will come, usually in the night, to run away from a cruel husband or father. We hide them."

"How do you survive? How do you feed yourselves, clothe yourselves?" I asked, my gaze straying to her dress for a moment.

"Not well, if that's what you mean!" she laughed again. "We fish in the river and set traps in the woods. Most of us are still wearing the clothing we escaped in. There's a fella' from downriver that comes up when he can and helps us with the buildings. Another one from our village that comes in the night with lumber he bought at the mill upriver and gives it to us, so long as we agree to not tell anyone he's helped us. We're getting by on kindness, mister."

I looked around at my Lightwalker fellows and saw steel in all of them.

I can't walk away from this. No decent person could.

The Voice didn't speak, but I felt it there, heavy as the hot sun on my shoulders.

"We have some kindness to spare. What can we help you with, ma'am?" I asked, dismounting.

We spent three days in the women's settlement. Osuin and Helm split enough wood to get them through the winter. Ishik and Eusebia taught the women how to hunt. Ishik's father had been a leatherworker, and she taught the women how to treat the animal skins and turn them into usable leather. I was reminded so strongly of Bettina and Hawthorne, I wouldn't have been surprised to see them come striding out of the forest alongside the women there.

They were a hardy bunch of twelve women, all between twenty and forty in age. They had iron-hard eyes and straight backs, but I could see the strain in their shoulders. What had happened to these women, to choose to live like this? Lightwalker women had equal say in their lives, at least as much as any man did. We all bowed equally to the elder council.

Their unspoken leader was the first woman we'd met, whose name was Calliope. It was a joyful sounding name for such a straight-laced woman. She handled me like a useful tool that had fallen into her lap unexpectedly. I was reminded of some of the small town magistrates I'd met among the downlanders. I expected that with her at the helm, these women would continue to survive.

"Do you Lightwalkers always do this kind of work for downlanders?" she asked me on the third day.

"No, ma'am," I answered. We were eating a stew of rabbit and wild onions. Someone had thought to bring salt with them when they ran, so the stew was flavored well. "But I try to offer a helping hand to anyone in need, if I can."

She was watching me eat, and I finished the bowl. Eusebia and Ishik had helped fill their larder with meat, so I knew they wouldn't starve to death any time soon.

"You don't know us," she said.

"Don't have to, do I?" I responded. She took up my bowl and spoon and shook her head.

"I had a husband, on the other side of the river. He died a year ago, a sickness that started in his lungs. I watched him cough himself to death," she said. She sat beside me. A healthy distance from us, Osuin and Helm were eating with a couple of the older women. Eusebia and Ishik were outside on the boardwalk with some of the younger women, teaching them Gods Above only knew what.

Where had Ashwin got to? I frowned. Probably snuck off to shed some light.

"I'm so sorry," I said to her. An itch to rise and leave started in my legs, but her eyes kept me in place.

"His family didn't like me. Said I was too outspoken. When he died, they took our home and kicked me out. Inside a week, I lost my husband, my home, and my livelihood. I had only ever been a wife to him. I knew how to cook and clean and care for a man, but nothing else. No one would hire me. I slept in the streets for two weeks, huddled under a mercy lamp outside the chapel."

I was horrified. She could have been hollowed! What kind of family would do that to a woman? Any woman?

She smiled, but it was a sad smile.

"I can see that you would let a stranger in your house before sending someone out in the dark alone," she said. "You're the good kind of man."

I swallowed. I didn't think basic kindness made me good. Just not a monster. These women had a different scale to judge by.

"And Ishik told me you have no wife of your own," she said, looking at me curiously. "I wonder why that is. You're handsome enough. Do you drink yourself into a stupor? Do you have a terrible temper that scares people? I can't believe it about you, but there must be something," she said.

I leaned away from her.

"Why would you ask about that?" I gaped.

"Because I no longer have a husband, and a place like this could use a good man or two," she said. I'd never heard of a downlander woman speaking so frankly to a stranger of any kind, much less a Lightwalker. I felt my ears go red, and she smiled at me.

"I, uhh…" I stammered. What on the land was I supposed to say to *that*?

"Our kind aren't allowed to marry downlanders, miss," said a voice at my shoulder. I looked up to find Ashwin there. He was grinning down at me like a cat that had caught a mouse. "And Cunigast here hasn't spent much time around women, if you know my meaning."

He winked at the woman and she smiled again.

"I could cure him of that," she said, eyeing me again.

Gods Above, I have to get out of here!

I opened my mouth to respond, but nothing came out. I was out of my depth, and she knew it.

"Thank you kindly for the offer, ma'am," I stammered, feeling my cheeks heat. "But I have to lead my team home tomorrow."

"You're always welcome to come back, Cunigast," she said again, looking me in the eye with not the slightest pinkening of her cheeks.

I rose and left, only barely refraining from running. Outside, the air was cool against my skin, a relief.

"What's got you so flustered?" Ishik asked from her spot on the boardwalk.

"That woman in there was threatening to eat him up!" Ashwin answered, exiting behind me. He was *laughing*, blight him!

Ishik laughed, too, but Eusebia looked stormy.

"She what?" Eusebia asked.

"Nothing. It's nothing," I stammered. Then, "I declined her offer."

"Yes, he was very polite about it," Ashwin said, striding forward to sit next to Ishik. "Think it scared him down to his moccasins."

Ishik and Ashwin were laughing a little *too* much, I decided. Eusebia wasn't laughing at all.

Osuin and Helm came clattering out of the little house I'd just been in, and looked at me sheepishly.

"Never seen a woman talk like *that* to anyone!" Helm said, and Osuin elbowed him hard in the ribs.

"Shut up!" Osuin said. "We weren't supposed to hear all that!"

Oh Gods Above, they'd heard the whole thing!

Helm's lips were trembling though.

"Sorry, Uncle Cunigast!" he said, barely holding back his own laughter, I realized. Osuin looked little better.

"At least she was a pretty one," Osuin muttered. "Better than the deal I was offered."

"Wait," I said, holding up a hand. "One of the women approached you, too?"

Osuin and Helm exchanged looks. "Both of us, actually. Nice girls, but not enough to tempt us, if you take my meaning."

"Me as well," Ashwin answered from Ishik's side. "I think they are trying to get men to come settle with them any way they can."

This was a surprise, but also a relief. Calliope had been so bold, maybe she was just doing what she believed was her duty.

Then I remembered her roving eyes, and the clear interest there. I felt my cheeks heat up again. *Maybe not* only *duty*.

"I can't believe they've been propositioning all of you boys, and haven't made an offer on Eusebia and me!" Ishik exclaimed, sounding indignant.

"They aren't likely to marry a lady, are they?" Osuin said, his tone dry.

"There are other ways to get people to settle in a place than marriage, boy," she said, snorting.

"Maybe someone should tell them that," Osuin said. Helm laughed, unable to contain himself.

"You should have seen Uncle Cunigast's face when that woman sat down beside him!" He fell down laughing on Ishik's other side. "I'd give anything to see that again!"

"Not me," Osuin said. "I was as embarrassed as he was."

Somehow, this did not make me feel any better.

"I suppose it was easy and casual when those women talked to you, then?" I glared at Helm, who was still laughing.

"It wasn't so bad," Helm said, smiling. "Nice girl saying she'd like to marry you. I could get used to that."

Ashwin was smiling, too. *He probably is used to it!*

I'd never given it much thought, but Ashwin was a good-looking man. Hair dark as night and taller than me. He had long-legs that ate up the ground. He probably would have had an easy time with women even without his light. My nephews as well. Helm was not quite as tall as me, but broad in the shoulders. He was strong and had an easy smile. Osuin, lankier and taller, was also quieter. He had Heva's dark coloring and I supposed he was what a woman might call handsome. I wondered if the girls in camp flirted with them or not. It wasn't the kind of thing I knew. I knew how good most of the girls were with a bow and arrow, or at horse-riding, but not who they might flirt with.

I realized that Ishik was right. I was painfully naive where women were concerned. It was unlikely to become a problem I had to face. I shrugged the thoughts off.

"Regardless of our offers, we'll all need to leave in the morning. If you have any last minute projects you're helping these women with, let's wrap it up tonight."

They each nodded understanding, and I turned on my heel. I had been fixing the roof on the last house on the row. A tree had fallen, and a branch had knocked a hole in it. With so few buildings, they needed every single one. Osuin had cleared the tree, but the roof was in a terrible state.

I scaled the side of the building easy enough. There wasn't much of an eave, so I pulled myself up and over. The roof was just wooden shingles nailed down over wooden beams. I wondered what they'd done to get nails. If nothing else, these women were resourceful.

I thought again of Calliope offering to marry me and shuddered. The idea of wedding a woman I didn't love repulsed me.

Looking behind me, I could just see Eusebia disappearing into the forest, likely to check her snares. I suppose she would know something about that. Marrying someone out of duty or survival. I turned and went back to nailing down roof shingles. The hammer blows couldn't drown out the thoughts circling my head.

Chapter Thirty-Eight

Calliope and the other women stood on the boardwalk and watched us ride away in the morning. Calliope's offer was still there, plain in her expression. I just tipped my head and mounted my horse with as much dignity as I could muster.

Ashwin winked at a girl as we left and I glared at him.

Was two women not enough? How could he dare encourage these women, destitute and living on the edge of life already? He caught my glare and laughed.

"Not all of us can live like you, Cunigast!" he declared. "Besides, I never touched her. You can stop giving me that fishy glare. My honor is intact, such that it is."

I didn't know what to say to that, either, so I snapped the reins along Obadiah's neck and he carried me forward until Ashwin and his troublesome behavior were behind me.

Eusebia had been in a stormy mood since finding out the women had been after us, but now she was lightening. She was sitting high on her horse, arms loose and a smile was turning the corners of her mouth up. She tilted her head back to look up at the canopy of trees. I watched her long hair sway loose behind her shoulders.

Osuin cleared his throat, and I realized he was riding beside me.

"Yes, Osuin?" I asked, switching my attention away from Eusebia and over to my nephew. He was tense across the shoulders, and seemed reluctant to meet my eyes.

I slowed my horse, letting the rest of the group pull ahead of us. Osuin took the cue gratefully, and watched the others pull farther and farther ahead. Once the last of the group rounded a bend in the trail and was out of sight, I looked at Osuin, waiting. He cleared his throat again, ducked his head once, and fidgeted with the bandana at his neck.

"Why can't we marry downlanders?" he asked.

"No one's told you before?"

I thought that was standard teaching among the elders. It was one of those deep rules of Lightwalker life, our otherness. We didn't take to outsiders, though much of our work was in service to them. After all, it wasn't for Lightwalkers that we took these endless runs south.

Osuin shook his head. "I guess they told us, but I just thought it was one of those things. You know, elders say all kinds of stuff. Can't say I put a lot of stock in most of it."

I smirked, knowing what he meant. "The elders don't tend to go on many runs, do they?"

"Not that I've seen," Osuin answered with a huff. It was a point of contention between the runners and the elders. Elders were making decisions about business they didn't partake in themselves. The compromise was that there was always a retired runner on the council, and a current runner present for any decisions about a fellow runner. Tor had stood up for more than just me over the years, playing a critical role in the community.

"Elders don't know a lot about downlanders, but they do know one thing."

Osuin's eyes finally met mine.

"Downlanders don't lightshare."

"Is that all it is?" he frowned.

"A Lightwalker alone among downlanders is destined to die, one way or another."

"And if a downlander came to live among our kind? What would be the harm in that?" he asked.

"Eh," I answered with a shrug. "Too many Lightwalker secrets, I suppose. The downlanders don't know a lot about us, and that's by design."

Osuin was quiet for a while, and we rode companionably in the silence for a stretch.

"Can't think of any secret that is worth all of this… separation," Osuin said, finally.

"Can't you?" I asked, raising an eyebrow. "I suppose it's not a secret, but it surely divided us."

"Othniel?" Osuin asked, his voice pitching higher. "That's the problem? A Lightwalker long dead?"

I just nodded. "Lot of these people are willing to die over Othniel's teachings. Do you think they're likely to convert any Lightwalkers? I doubt we're going to be able to turn them to our way of thinking."

Osuin huffed again. "More like tell them the truth. That's a secret that needs spilling."

"I agree," I said, and Osuin's eyes grew round. Most elders viewed the downlander religion based on one of our kind as a deception the downlanders had put on themselves. It wasn't our responsibility to correct a mistake we hadn't made.

But Othniel, himself, had been our responsibility. Hadn't he?

"Besides," I added. "There's always the risk of accidental lightsharing with a downlander. You know what that would mean."

"We just spent three days with downlanders, and no one burst from it," Osuin said, shrugging some more. "I don't accidentally lightshare with Lightwalkers. What makes a downlander any different?"

"What's got you thinking about this, anyway?" I asked, setting aside the prickly issue of Othniel's legacy and downlander safety. "Were you more tempted than you let on by the offer of one of those nice girls back there?"

Osuin straightened. "Not so much. They were nice girls, but it takes more than a day or two to convince me of anything."

I smiled, knowing that was true. Osuin was slow to come to his decisions, and hard to move once he got there. Helm would have been a much more likely candidate.

"Then what? Have you met a downlander girl somewhere else, and I just didn't notice?" I was teasing him.

"It's just been gnawing at me, I guess," Osuin said. He made a swipe at his hair, and I realized he was blushing. "Since we met that woman Bettina and her son, Hawthorne. Just seemed like there should have been more we could have done for them. I got to thinking, if you could have brought her home with you all those years ago, the first time you met her..." Osuin let his voice trail off, and he looked away with a shrug.

I couldn't deny that Bettina and her boy had been on my mind since our visit as well. When I'd rescued her from her captors all those years ago, my head had been too full of Eusebia to give her much thought then. But now? Years later, knowing how she'd clung to survival on the edge of civilization all these years. Yes, she'd been on my mind.

But bring a downlander girl back to Iron Camp? Gods Above, that would be a much worse life, surely! She would have never been welcomed into the work-a-day life of the Lightwalkers. What would that leave? Keeping house, alone, in someone's cabin? Likely mine, I realized with a shudder.

No. That's no life.

"I understand what you mean," I said, struggling for something to say. "But what kind of life would Bettina have had with us? Do you think she'd be welcome in the square? Do you think the women would have befriended her? She would never be allowed to marry. What kind of life do you think that would be for someone? Anyone?"

"Not much different than the one she's had, Uncle Cunigast," Osuin answered. The words were a punch in the chest, hammering against the cage around my heart.

I thought about those women we'd just left behind. How different would their lives be, if instead of hammering down some shingles, I'd loaded them up and brought them home with me?

Gods Above! It was unfathomable!

Wasn't it?

"Maybe you're right, Osuin," I said. "But I can't imagine it happening any time soon, all the same."

I rode the rest of the day wondering if Osuin expected too much, or if I didn't expect enough.

Chapter Thirty-Nine

We retraced our steps without incident. I watched Osuin and Helm improve with each passing day. Gods Above, they were magnificent! I couldn't wait to tell Heva about them. She would glow with pride, and rightly so.

On an open plain, I watched Helm take down a bird in flight with only his light. It was an impressive cut, though overshadowed by the sight of Eusebia standing on her running horse's back and taking down two more with arrows. Ishik rolled her eyes and laughed.

"Let the boys have their moment, Eusebia!" she called. Osuin was so shocked at the sight of her, he missed catching the falling birds. Shee circled his horse on the plain, and picked them up without dismounting- another riding trick.

I laughed, too. The sight of Osuin and Helm's open mouths was too ridiculous. Beside me, Ashwin smiled. I knew that he could outshine all of us combined, and therefore be the most impressive on the field. But he didn't. Instead, he gave me a knowing smile and volunteered to clean the birds for our dinner.

"I'll help," Ishik said, dismounting alongside Ashwin. "I haven't done anything else to earn my keep today, and I'm certainly not going to trick-ride to keep up with that lot!"

We settled in at the edge of the plain for the night. I gathered firewood from the surrounding forest, whistling. It was a good day. Easy riding, kind weather, no sign of breachers on the trail. We had stopped and spoken to some downlanders at a narrow point in the river. Boatmen on their flat-bottomed boats shored up for some fishing. They had no stories of shadow creatures besides the common kind. Tension bled out of my chest that I hadn't realized was there.

"What's got you in such a good mood?" a voice called behind me.

Eusebia. She was picking her way through the trees, following my trail. I watched her with a full heart, but no guilt.

"What are you doing?" I asked. I hefted another piece of wood from the forest floor, and watched as she drew near.

"Thought I'd help gather firewood," she said, then paused. "You're not still avoiding me, are you?"

"No." It was the honest truth. I'd felt no reason to avoid being alone with her since that last conversation.

"Good." She bent to pick up a fallen branch, likely knocked down in a recent storm.

"Eusebia," I said, picking my moment carefully. "There's something I want to give you."

Straightening, she frowned. I stepped closer and set my firewood aside. I took what little she'd gathered and set it atop my own pile.

"What is it, Cunigast?" she asked.

I pulled the knife, sheath and all, from my belt and handed it to her, hilt-first.

"Heva made it for me," I said. "I'd like for you to have it."

Her fingers touched the hilt, then hesitated.

"What does this mean to you, Cunigast?" she asked, tilting her head up to look into my eyes.

I paused.

"It does mean something, doesn't it?" she prodded gently.

"It does," I answered. "But maybe not what you think."

Eusebia waited, not yet taking the knife. I rubbed my thumb across the leather sheath.

"She intended it to go to a fiance, which of course I never got," I said. "But really, it was meant to be a gift to someone important to me. Family, maybe. Or a light partner."

"But you aren't giving it to Ashwin." Her brow furrowed.

"I think it'd only be a burden to Ashwin," I said, turning away from her. "It's hard to explain. He already carries so much. He doesn't need to add me to his lists of cares."

"You think he'd be burdened by you?" Eusebia asked, circling around to look me in the eye again. "I thought you were like brothers."

"We are," I said quickly. "Like I said... it's hard to explain."

"Cunigast, you know that I have nothing to give you," she said. "Nothing of value, anyway."

I smiled at her, though it was a hard one. "I'm not looking for anything from you, Eusebia. This is different. This is..." my voice trailed off, trying to think of the right words.

Help would be nice right about now, I thought. The Voice was silent.

"I suppose this is just to signify between us. You know how I feel about you. I know how you feel about me. I don't expect anything to change. But this makes it...real."

I met her eyes, and handed her the knife again.

She took it, her fingers tightening around the handle. She understood, then.

"I will take this for now," she said. "But I suspect it should eventually go to someone else."

"Who else will there ever be?" I asked, seriously. "There has only ever been you."

Eusebia sighed, and I wasn't sure if it was in frustration or relief.

"I only mean that I can't *really* be family to you, and we both know that. So, I'm only keeping this for you. I'm a placeholder until the right person finally comes. Do you understand?" she asked, her eyes shining. "You deserve the real thing. I'll hold this knife until the real thing comes along for you."

I blinked back tears, and gripped her hand, the knife between us.

"Keep it for as long as you like," I said. I picked up the firewood, hers and mine, and walked back to camp.

Chapter Forty

My eyes snapped open.

What is it?

Get up. Now. Run.

I rolled to my feet, glancing around the camp. I counted Ishik and Eusebia, rolled up tight into their bedrolls. Ashwin was there, sprawled haphazardly across his blankets.

The boys.

A glance at the sky told me it was Helm's watch, but I knew that sometimes they sat through both of their watches together.

I started running. Eyes searching, I aimed myself at a cold knot of silence in the forest.

Whatever it is, let me get there in time!

Legs pumping, I dodged around trees and brush, leaping over fallen branches like a deer.

The silence was spreading, the coldness a palpable feeling in my chest.

Then there were soft sounds of bodies moving, and I put on a burst of speed.

Osuin and Helm were fighting a handful of rivermen, scuffling in the dark. I saw knives flashing and went for my own. Two men fell in quick succession. I threw myself into the fray without thinking.

Fists and feet, scrambling in the dirt. Lightwalkers spent their lives training, not to fight, but to *dodge*. Contact with a breacher was deadly, and the goal was never to let one touch you, anywhere. Osuin and Helm were fighting honorably, and I thought we could turn the tide.

A large man was grappling with me, clearly superior in strength and size. But I had a canny way of breaking a hold, and I broke his, pushing him down like a tree with a hook of my foot behind his ankle.

There was a cry. I spun around.

Osuin was down, blood pumping out from between his hands where they clutched a knife buried in his chest.

"Osuin!" I shouted. Helm was fighting to get to him. I was doing the same, but a sea of bodies separated us.

I watched him fall back, his eyes searching the sky. Light filtered up through his fingers, but with the knife lodged in place, he couldn't heal.

An arm jerked me back, one around my throat and another buried in my hair. I kicked hard, turning my hips to throw my attacker over. It didn't work. Another set of hands had my arms, pinning me back.

I began to thrash. I had to get to Osuin. If we could remove the knife, Helm could lightshare-

"Uncle!" Helm shouted. He was on his stomach, another riverman on his back. The knife was already in him when my eyes found him.

Digging in my feet, I roared and threw myself backward. The men holding me crashed down with me. Kicking my feet, I scrambled away from them, but another knife was at the ready.

I felt steel slide into my ribs. The pain sliced me in half, and what little light I had surged to mend the breach.

"Told you!" one of the men growled. "You have to leave the knife in 'em!"

My eyes rolled, and I struggled to focus. I coughed, and my lips were wet with blood.

Lungs. The knife had punctured a lung. I was dying.

How could you let this happen? I demanded of The Voice. Then, *please! Not like this!*

I heard more thrashing. The hands that held me lessened, then disappeared. I was lying flat, somewhere, the world dark around me.

"Cunigast, don't you dare die on me!" There was growling near my ear and I thought it was another riverman, trying to prolong my death.

A flash of light, a burning sensation all through the core of my body.

I gasped, sat upright.

"Enough!" Eusebia shouted. "That's enough, Ashwin!"

Ashwin? I'd forgotten all about him in the scuffle. And Eusebia? What was she doing here?

I pushed back my hair and raised my head.

"Osuin! Helm!" I shouted, scrambling past Ashwin and Eusebia's white faces.

Ishik was bent over their bodies, tears streaming down her face. A sound was coming out of her that I'd never heard before. Wailing, I suppose it was.

I fell to my knees, hands reaching for them. Osuin and Helm were lying side-by-side. Their eyes stared sightlessly up at the night sky. The knives were gone from their bodies, but it was clear that they were dead.

Too late. I'd been *too late*.

I sucked in a breath. I didn't know how I'd ever breathe again.

"Boys," I whispered. Hands shaking, I closed their eyes.

Helm had never been quite as dark as his brother. Together, they were like looking at a pair of hunting birds, felled in their prime.

Why did you let this happen? I thought. Then, *why didn't you wake me sooner?*

Too late, I was too late.

Hands were on my shoulders, drawing me back. Eusebia and Ashwin drug me away. It wasn't until then that I realized I'd been saying the words out loud.

Gods Above, I'd been screaming it.

All around the forest were bodies of rivermen with arrows sprouting from their chests. Ishik and Eusebia had done their deadly work, and saved my life. Ashwin, too. But it hadn't been enough. It hadn't been fast enough.

My nephews were dead.

"We have to bury them, Cunigast," Ashwin was saying. There were tears on his cheeks. Eusebia had her arms around me, pulling me back against her chest. I wasn't sure if it was for comfort or restraint.

"They can't be dead," I said. "They can't be!"

"Cunigast," Ashwin said, stern and slow. "We. Have. To. Bury. Them."

I swallowed hard. Surely not. Surely there was no way their lives could be cut so short so suddenly.

There hadn't even been a breacher. I choked.

There hadn't even been a breacher!

Chapter Forty-One

The morning sun rose watery and cool over the forest as Ashwin and I finished burying my nephews. My cheeks were stiff with dried tears, but I was past weeping. I was silent all the way down to my bones.

Eusebia and Ishik stood at our sides, having gathered all of our belongings. Ishik had a fair voice and she sang an old Lightwalker song for them. They all looked at me to say a few words, but I found there was nothing in me to say.

"It shouldn't have happened," I said simply. Then, down to the boys, "I would have gladly given all the light in my body to save even one of you."

I walked away, leaving Ashwin and the others to say whatever they would. My nephews deserved far better than this humble grave not twenty steps from the bodies of their murderers.

I looked the men over. There was nothing notable about any of them, except that each had a red string tied around their upper arms. Common downlander rivermen that had more business on a fishing boat than tangling with Lightwalkers in the darkness.

What on the land had sent them out on this grisly quest?

"I suppose we'll have to bury them as well," Ashwin said, from somewhere behind me.

I was angry. It was a familiar feeling. I'd spent so much of my youth angry, it was like welcoming back an old lover. The anger settled in my chest and I found it an easier burden than my grief.

"No," I said. "I'll not bury a one of them."

"We can't just leave them here," Ashwin said. "Can we?"

I turned, a coldness settling itself over my bones, and gripped the knife still at my waist.

"No. I have a better idea."

Eusebia frowned at me, as if she didn't recognize me.

"Help me drag them to the river," I said to Ashwin.

"Cunigast-"

"That's an order!" I snapped.

Don't do this.

I didn't hesitate. I hooked one dead man under the shoulders and began dragging him. I didn't look to see if Ashwin helped. I'd drag them all myself, if I had to.

A cumbersome haul toward the river revealed what I knew it would. There were three boats pulled up on the shore, all empty except for a yellow dog, barking at us.

I hoisted the man's body onto the nearest boat and started back for another. Ashwin was behind me, a second body over his shoulder.

Ashwin and I took an hour to get them all to the boat, filling it with its gruesome burden. Somewhere along the way, the dog gave up barking.

"What are you going to do now?" Ishik asked, watching from the shore, pale as the fog rising off the river.

"I'm going to return these men home," I said. "Help me push off."

Stop.

If you didn't want this to happen, you should have woken me up sooner!

I jumped onto the boat, poling it away from the shore. Ashwin stood on the shore with the women, and helped push it out, wading into the water up to his knees. By then, I had it going.

I pulled a tinderbox from my pocket and set the boat alight. Walking around, I lit it in a few places. At the very least, the boat would burn down to the waterline. After that? Who knew?

Once it was burning well, I jumped into the water and swam back. I didn't care what the water did to my clothes, my belongings. As far as I was concerned, I was as dead as Helm and Osuin.

The dog jumped out behind me, and swam to the bank.

"Let's go," I said, striding up onto the bank. The others stared at me, alternating between the burning boat slowly floating downriver, and the water streaming off of my clothes.

"You'll start a war!" Eusebia exclaimed.

"I'll fight it, too," I answered coolly. "Mount up. I want to be out of here before they come back looking for the other boats."

Silence. I met their eyes, one after the other, daring them to argue with me.

"If there is to be a war, they started it," Ashwin said. I nodded at him, one quick jerk of my head, and went to find my horse. The yellow dog stayed on the bank, keeping vigil over his dead owners.

The others fell into step behind me, but the silence followed us all the way home.

Chapter Forty-Two

I delivered Eusebia and Ishik back to their families, and reported to the elder council with the animation of a rock at the bottom of a mine.

I walked down the lane toward Heva's home with lead in my mocassins. How on the land was I going to tell her?

She met me on the path, already crying. Roderic was at her side, looking pale and brittle.

How did they know? No one else knew.

"I'm sorry, Heva," I said, wooden, my body too exhausted to weep anymore.

Heva slumped in the middle of the path, Roderic beside her. She wasn't looking at me, and I was ashamed that it was a relief. I couldn't meet her eyes, I could barely look at her at all.

"I'm so sorry, sister," I said again, then turned and walked away.

Ashwin met me on the path, running.

"What?" I asked, frowning.

"Trouble. Elder lodge."

I ran alongside him, as he explained between breaths.

There was some debate over whether Helm and Osuin's name should be put on the wall. They had died on a run, but not fighting a breacher. There had been accidents in the past, but never had a Lightwalker died in an outright fight with a downlander. This level of violence had never happened in memory, and there was no known precedence.

I shoved open the doors of the elder council lodge, Ashwin quick on my heels.

"You'll put their name on the wall, or you'll build a new wall!" I growled, silencing them mid-sentence.

Ashwin put his hand on my shoulder, but I shook it off.

"You'll not dishonor them! They died fighting!" I snapped, turning from Ashwin back to the elders. "They didn't die from falling off a horse or drowning in the river! Do you hear me?"

I slammed my hands down on the table where they were gathered.

"They didn't die fighting a breacher, though," one man said. He looked old enough to be my grandfather and hadn't been on a run since his first and only run as a youngster.

"No," I said, lowering my voice. "There were no breachers around. My nephews trained all their lives to fight breachers and in the end common rivermen put a knife in their bodies and held them down until they died of the wound. Osuin was trying to heal himself to survive long enough for Helm to get to him. Helm died trying to fight his way to his brother, a knife in his back. I should have died," I said. The words choked me.

"I should have died."

"But you didn't," the elder said simply.

I lunged, but was pulled up short by Ashwin's arms dragging me back. He held me against his chest, arms pinned at my sides.

"No, Cunigast didn't die," Ashwin said over my shoulder. "But he had a knife buried into his left lung, was coughing up blood, and it still took four rivermen to hold him down. He was still fighting to get to Osuin and Helm when Ishik and Eusebia and I rained arrows down on the rivermen and saved him. If we'd arrived ten seconds earlier, Cunigast would have likely saved both of his nephews."

There was silence in the room. I shook Ashwin off, trying to catch my breath and tamp down the fury raging through me.

"But they didn't die fighting breachers," another elder, this one a woman, said helplessly. She spread her hands wide as if uncertain what else to say.

"They died fighting a war we didn't know we were in. If that's not level with fighting a breacher, I don't know what is."

I turned and left, unable to bear what else they might say.

In the end, the elders erected another wall. It was smaller than the ancestral original. The stones of this wall were of more human dimensions, but they tried to make it as impressive as they could with such inferior means.

I stood in the square and watched their names go on the new wall. The whole of Iron Camp came to watch, an uncertain tremor passing from person to person. Heva and Roderic lit the brazier for both boys and stood watch. I stood there as well, though I let them stand in the place of honor.

Heva hadn't spoken to me since I'd delivered the news so poorly. I didn't know what she had been told of their deaths, but I couldn't bring myself to relay the details to her. For myself, I could see nothing else but their deaths over and over when I closed my eyes. It was a horror, and I couldn't believe knowing it would bring my sister comfort.

Eusebia, Ishik and Ashwin came for the lighting of the brazier. Ashwin stood on one side of me and Eusebia stood on the other. They both kept watch with me the first night. After that, the three of them seemed to have some agreement to check on me in turns.

The brazier's light died out on the fourth day. Heva and Roderic were staggering under their exhaustion when they left. They still had other children to care for.

I stayed.

I sat in the square, oblivious of the work resuming all around me. People passed around me in a wide berth. There was something so cruel about that brazier going cold. I couldn't walk away. If I did, it would all be over.

The fifth day, Ashwin sat beside me, and didn't leave when I expected him to. He didn't say anything. I was glad. I couldn't speak.

He set his hand on my shoulder and shared just enough to keep me alive.

On the sixth day, it began to rain. Ashwin had left long enough to sleep for the night, and he returned with the rain.

Eusebia came as well, settling an oilcloth cloak over my shoulders. She sat for a while, tears on her cheeks, but left again.

Some part of me knew that this wasn't helping. Osuin and Helm were just as dead, no matter how long I moldered here in the square. I wondered how long I could stay here, before someone forced me back to my empty cabin.

In the end, it was Lasha who got me moving.

I hadn't seen her arrive in the square. She settled herself down in front of me, that silly raccoon on her shoulder.

"Cunigast, boy," she said. The sternness was somewhat lessened by the tears standing in her eyes. "You have to go on."

"I can't, Lasha," I answered. My voice was rusty from disuse. "I can't let them go."

Lasha reached forward, one hand on my shoulder.

"They are already gone. It's only you here. They wouldn't want this, even if they were here."

Lasha and Ashwin walked me home, and Lasha tucked me into my bed as if I were a child. When I woke the next morning, Lasha had gone home, but Ashwin was still sitting in my cabin, watching the sun rise through the window.

"Eusebia sent food," he said. "She said she'll knock you out herself if you don't eat."

I huffed, not quite a laugh. Then, I put my face in my hands and cried. I would never see my nephews again.

Two days later, Ashwin was still living in my cabin with me. I looked up from my place on the porch and looked at him. He was sitting on the steps, watching the sun rise. My sense of day and night were disordered. I slept badly and rose at odd hours. I knew it could not go on forever.

"When will you go back home?" I asked. Ashwin glanced over at me and away again.

"I won't," he answered.

"What do you mean?" I asked, perking up. It was the first time something that was not my nephews had caught my attention.

"Minette asked for our marriage to be dissolved."

I gaped. "She asked for it? When?"

It was far more customary for the council to initiate such a thing. If I was honest, I was surprised that they hadn't done it years ago. There were no children.

"When we rode out on this last run. I was going to tell you when we got back," he shrugged.

"Tell me what to say to you," I said.

"Don't have to say anything at all. It's just what happened."

"So now you're a free man," I said. "Laela-"

"No."

I was shocked. Surely they would get married now?

"The council already said no. They'll give me someone else. Some other poor woman."

Ashwin was tearing blades of grass apart with his fingers and flicking them out into the yard.

"I'm sorry, Ashwin."

He tossed the last of the grass in his hands down and stood.

"Why?" he asked. "Nothing will change."

I swallowed whatever words were rising up in my throat. I'd given my knife to Eusebia. I had no room to speak.

Instead, I listened to his footsteps as he retreated into the cabin.

I looked out at the yard that was lightening with the sunrise. There was a soft fog dissolving before my eyes.

You left us alone. How could you?

I'd been asking some variation of this of The Voice since Osuin and Helm had died. There had been no answer, only a chilling silence that left me devoid of hope. The breath in my body felt like a punishment. I would have gladly given up my life. I'd thought about it, in fact. How easy would it be to simply walk into the forest after dark? Canny as ever, Ashwin slept in front of the door.

Rising to my feet, I stepped off the porch and began walking into the forest. I didn't have a clear destination in mind, but I wasn't surprised to find myself, some moments later, atop the waterfall.

I looked down at the shallow basin of water. The riverbed here was wet, as the mountains released their snowy burden and the waterfall was churning away. I stood, watching the water freefall down, down, down...

My toes found the edge of the cliff, and I leaned forward.

Sunlight glinted on the water. It misted into the air, wetting my skin and causing my hair to stick at my temples.

It would be so easy to keep leaning. For that brief moment, would I feel free? Would it be a relief?

Or would I regret it?

Wait.

I sucked in a breath and stumbled backward.

"What for?" I shouted. "What am I waiting for this time?"

Heva had no children waiting to be born. Eusebia was married. Ashwin would find another light partner. The only people who had a use for me had died on my watch.

"What could I possibly be waiting for this time?" I asked, and sobbed. The rocks were hard under my knees, but I didn't feel them. Gods Above, I wished I could feel something other than the aching in my chest!

There are still those that need you.

"Where? Where are these people you think need me?" I demanded. I was so tired. I was tired of hurting. Tired of the loneliness. Tired of the anger.

You promised Heva.

There was a shaking that had started in my center and had radiated outward. I was trembling from head to toe like a leaf in a winter wind. Some part of me longed for the cliff's edge, but I knew The Voice was right about one thing: I had promised Heva I wouldn't kill myself.

On shaking legs, I climbed back down from the cliff and out of the forest. I hadn't decided to go see Heva, wasn't sure I *could ever* go see her again. When I crossed out of the forest path and neared my own cabin, she was already there, waiting as if The Voice had told her where I was.

"Sister," I said. She had more grey in her hair than I remembered, and she looked as if she'd lost weight.

"Cunigast," she said back. We stood on the path, separated by a short distance and stared at each other.

"I don't know what to say," I said, finally. "No amount of sorries could ever make up for what you've lost."

Her face tightened, but her eyes were still clear.

"What you've lost as well, brother."

"Aye," I answered. "What I've lost as well."

"What will you do now?" she asked.

I looked away. What *would* I do?

"I don't know."

"They would want you to keep fighting breachers. They would want you to learn why this happened to them."

I met her eyes. "You want me to fight downlanders, then. Not breachers."

"You are out in the world more than most. You tell me. What's happening out there?" she asked, and there was steel in her voice.

I faltered. What did I know?

"Those rivermen... they each wore red strings tied around their arms."

"What does that mean?"

"I don't know, I ..." I stopped.

"You do know, don't you?" she said, stepping closer. She put a hand to my arm and I looked down at her. "What do they mean?"

"Hathas," I said.

I doubted she knew what that name meant any more than she knew what red strings meant. Regardless, she nodded her head and squeezed my arm.

"You'll know better than anyone," she said. "Go up to the elder lodge. They are discussing what happened, but none of them were there."

"I wasn't invited, Heva-"

"Aren't you listening?" she demanded, her voice the closest to a shout that I'd ever heard. "None of them were there. My sons died and they are making decisions, but *none of them were there!*"

Her eyes seared into mine.

"Tell Ashwin where I've gone," I said and ran down the path toward the square and the elder lodgehouse. I didn't wait to see if she would do what I said or not.

I had always been fairly quick, and now I was fueled with anger and grief and hurt. I flew down the path. I was used to being ignored and undervalued by my community, but I wouldn't let that happen to Osuin and Helm's memory.

The people in the square split like the pages in a book as I crossed it. Each person seemed to pull away from me, and I was reminded of my youth, when they wouldn't even look at me.

I looked now, facing these people who'd been the only people I'd known my whole life. I expected to find disgust there.

Instead, I found fear. People, even men, were drawing away as if I might set them alight if they drew too close.

I was shocked. What did they have to fear from me?

I stepped up the grey stone steps of the elder lodgehouse, and paused with my hand on the door. There was a metal plate on the door that read "Iron Camp" in broad letters. It had been shined up to mirror brightness and I could see my own face reflected back.

Suddenly, I understood why grown men recoiled from me.

I looked angry.

The shadow of my father stared back at me from under stormy brows and dark eyes. My long hair was loose and blew around me in a spring breeze. In the grey metal mirror, I looked like a tornado that had taken on flesh. The anger was vibrating off of me in palpable sheets.

I gritted my teeth, and pulled the door open.

Whatever was on the other side of this door, whoever was there, I would face it. I would be relentless. Gods Above help whoever stood in my way.

Continue reading for a preview of the first book in the series, *Lightwalkers*…

A loud sound from inside the chapel pulled me out of my thoughts, and my head turned to listen. I heard footsteps coming at a quick pace. Alarm sizzled through my veins, and I looked down at helpless Sparrow on the ground.

"Let's get you up, Sparrow," I said, and levered his body up and against my own. His arms went around my neck, his clubbed hands hooked there stiffly. I scooped his long legs up in one arm and together we went toward the spindly cedar trees. There wasn't much cover, but it was the best I could do.

Instead of trouble, it was Hemlock, his arms pumping furiously. Eoghan was fast on his heels.

"Leave the boy, Acantha!" Hemlock whisper-shouted. "We must go! Now!"

"But Sparrow!" I called back. How could I leave him here alone? What if he fell? What if he hurt himself?

"Nevermind him now, girl!" Hemlock said, taking Sparrow out of my arms with his own. He propped Sparrow against the bench, and checked his twisted legs once.

"We must be gone, and quick about it!" Hemlock said, his face like a thundercloud. The old man had never hit me, in all the five years I'd lived with him, but for the first time it looked like he might.

"What's going on, Hemlock?" I asked, frozen. Hemlock grabbed my arm and began pulling me down the path. I stumbled once, then twice, and twisted my arm out of his grip.

"Stop! Enough!" I shouted, anger and confusion swelling up in my chest. "Tell me what's happening!"

Hemlock and Eoghan both turned to face me on the path, and I saw at once that they wore the same expression. Hemlock wasn't angry at all. He was afraid.

"I'll tell you at the house. Now go! Run!" Hemlock hissed between his teeth. Eoghan had gathered my things, shoving them unceremoniously in the basket, and tugging on one of my hands.

"What on the land is going on?" I asked, but Hemlock was already moving again, once again towing me alongside him. Eoghan dropped my hand and ran ahead of us down the path.

The house rose up to meet us on the path ahead. I could see that Eoghan had beat us by quite a bit, and was even now shutting the chickens up in the coop.

"Inside the house!" Hemlock shouted.

"But the chickens?" Eoghan called.

"Hang the chickens!" Hemlock shouted back, and Eoghan scrambled to get out of the coop. Stupidly, all I could think about was the clear inch of ankle visible at the bottom of my brother's trousers. I had let the hems out only a month ago. We'd have to ask Hemlock to buy us new clothes. Again.

I followed my mentor inside, and set my hands on my hips.

"Want to tell me what this is about, Hemlock?" I asked, keeping my voice firm. The old man was scaring me.

He spun on his heel and tossed his medicine bag in his chair. His hands went to his eyes, rubbing them, then pulled off the scarf he wore even in summer.

"Acantha, you have to take your brother and go."

I felt the words like a hit to my middle for the second time that day. I willed myself to stay standing tall, though I wanted to crumple like a doll.

"What?" Eoghan was behind me. I heard the crack in his voice and felt it as if my bones were cracking instead. "Did we do something wrong?"

We'll be homeless again.

"No, no," Hemlock said, waving his hands around. "I'm not kicking you out. You've done nothing wrong. God on the Land, you've never done anything that made me want to be rid of either of you…" Hemlock's eyes squeezed shut.

"Then what?" I asked, trying to firm myself up for whatever he said next.

"I'm trying to get you out of here alive!" Hemlock said. He stepped forward. Had he been a different kind of man, he might have taken my hands, or hugged us both. Instead, he stood there, wringing his hands in front of him.

"Eoghan heard it the same as I did," he said, but Eoghan looked as bewildered as I did.

"What happened at chapel?" I asked.

"That red-robed idiot was going on about witches coming to their power when they turned seventeen…" Hemlock's voice continued, but I could hear nothing except the pounding in my ears.

"What's that to do with us?" Eoghan asked, still lost.

"Today is Acantha's birthday, boy. Her seventeenth birthday," Hemlock answered, rubbing his balding head as he spoke. "And I'll not be the only one to remember it."

Glossary

Ashwin- Cunigast's light partner for years, from a camp over the mountains (snow camp)

Bettina-downlander girl Cunigast saves on his first run

Breacher- a shadow creature that has evolved to hold shape and manipulate mass

Brother Horatio- the contact in Othnio of the priest in Bettina's village

Brother Panuel- last white-robed priest in the no-name village nearest Iron Camp

Calliope- leader of the women's settlement on the East side of the river.

Chickadee- Lasha's horse

Church of Othniel- the downlander religion based on a Lightwalker

Colias- Cunigast's first light partner

Copper Camp- a Lightwalker camp disbanded around 30 years ago

Cunigast- the main character of this novel

Da- Cunigast's father, a knifemaker in Iron Camp

Daybreaker, or Breaker- a shadow creature that has evolved enough to appear in daylight

Elder Council- the governing group of every Lightwalker camp

Eusebia- a girl in Iron Camp and Cunigast's love interest

Gareth- Osuin's first light partner

Gods Above- the collective name for the gods that Lightwalkers believe in, also a common exclamation

Hawthorne- Bettina's son

Helm-Heva's second oldest son

Hemlock- downlander bonesetter in the no-name village nearest Iron Camp

Heva- Cunigast's older sister

Hathas- downlander priest preaching against Lightwalkers

Ishik- Eusebia's light partner, Pilan's sister

Laela- younger girl who goes on her first run with Cunigast and Ashwin, hurts her leg badly

Lasha- Tor's wife, also an experienced runner

Minette- Ashwin's wife

Nanook- Lasha's pet raccoon

Naomi- Eusebia's light partner on her first run

Nika- Laela's Light partner

Obadiah- Cunigast's horse

Osuin- Heva's oldest son

Othniel- a Lightwalker that the downlander religion is based on

Othnio-a large downlander city and the base of the Church of Othniel

Pilan- Eusebia's husband

Rada- Heva's oldest daughter and third child

Rhea- an experienced runner

Roderic- Heva's husband

Serg- a member of the elder council while Cunigast is a child

Shadow Creatures- the deadly, amorphous creatures that appear in darkness.

Shelly- Lightwalker in camp that makes exceptionally good medicinals for the horses

Silvan- an experienced runner

The Voice- unknown voice that only Cunigast can hear

Tor- an experienced runner, Cunigast goes on many runs with him

Currency

Copper coinies

Silver hats

Gold tops

Units of measurement

Pes (a roman foot)

Pace (approximately 5 feet)

Plethron (approximately 100 feet)

League (the distance an average person could walk in a day)

Acknowledgements

Acknowledgements for a self-published author are always a little awkward. I'm my own editor, formatter, cover artist and marketer (such that I am). The product you hold in your hands is almost entirely my own work with the exception of the platform that publishes it for me. And believe me, I am thankful beyond belief to get it to you.

My first thanks always go to my husband. My first beta-reader, guardian of my writing time, biggest fan and supporter, and the hauler of so many boxes at events, I could literally do none of this without him. Also, without him, I doubt I could write about the relationships between men and women with any sort of accuracy. Because of my dear husband, I know what it means to love someone, and to be loved in return. Like Cunigast, I know what it means to be chosen. I'm thankful for that more than I can say.

I also want to give many happy thanks to the crew of people who beta-read this novel on very short notice. My deep apologies for rushing you. I really thought this book was going to be published *much* sooner!

Julianna Robnett, who has beta-read every book I've written to date. How could I publish without you? I couldn't, I'm sure. Brett Nelson, who did war with adverbs on my behalf. I appreciated every comment you left, even if they made me want to hide on occasion. Jennette Gahlot, who is better at selling my books without a cover than I am with them. Ha! Ashley Hassell, who read the book in a few days without batting an eye. As if putting a book away in a few days is even a *challenge* for you! DaLayna Lincks, who has shared so many of my poor marketer's posts. I'm the marketer. It's my posts. I promise, I'll get better at this. And last but not least, Bill Wilwers, who encouraged me to use *less* exclamation points. I did try.

Though they will likely never know about it, I'd like to also thank the band The Crane Wives. I have listened to their music on repeat while writing everything in the Lightwalkers world. In particular, *Take Me To War* and *The Moon Will Sing*.

Additionally, I would like to thank Lois McMaster Bujold, who will also likely never see this. She wrote a series called *The Sharing Knife,* which was a significant influence in my writing these books. While my work is my own, there are some little tributes to that other series. It's meant as my way of honoring that influence.

And finally, I would like to thank you, the readers. Without you, I'd just be a wild woman, huddling in corners with a computer or notebook on my own. Because of you, they let me out on occasion. It's very kind of you to keep supporting me in that way!

I originally intended to write a short novella about Cunigast, as a kind of bonus story to Athan and Acantha's. Then I looked up at 60 thousand words, realized I was nowhere close to the end of his story and had accidentally started a war. *Sigh.* These things happen. The good news, though, is that there is another book coming. I'm already hard at work on it! Thank you for hanging in there with me while I work!

About the Author

Jacquelyn Holmes is a mom, wife, occasional ukulele player and largely unsuccessful gardener. She enjoys living in the south where it is rarely below freezing, sewing things no one asked for, and eating copious amounts of gluten-filled foods. She is the author of the *Native Legends series,* as well as *Lightwalkers: Athan and Acantha, volume one.* She also has a blog about weird, old books that is called "Weird Old Books." You can find that on her website as well.

Check out her website for more books
www.JacquelynHolmesBooks.com

Follow her on social media!
Facebook @authorjacquelynholmes
Instagram @author_jacquelyn